The Time Stealer

A Light Riders Novel

A Time Travel Mystery
by
Ann I. Goldfarb

Also by this author:

The Face Out of Time
Ripple Rider: An Anguillan Adventure in Time
The Last Tag

The Light Riders Series:
Light Riders and the Morenci Mine Murder
Light Riders and the Fleur-de-lis Murder
Light Riders and the Missouri Mud Murder
The Time Borrower

Praise for *The Time Stealer:*

"It's unusual to find science fiction, young adult protagonists, and history blending together so seamlessly; but the atmosphere, politics, culture, and concerns of ancient Greece come to life under Goldfarb's practiced hand and not only link into the other series titles, but create a fine mystery driven by two memorable, well-developed teen characters. *The Time Stealer's* ability to juxtapose multiple worlds is one hallmark of excellence that succeeds in immersing readers of all ages in its vivid story line. Read the story: it won't disappoint!"

Diane Donovan,
MIDWEST BOOK REVIEW

"For anyone who has been following this amazing time traveling series, you will be ecstatic to read this one! Once again this fun, unique author takes us back to a time that we can only imagine; a time of danger, darkness, and warriors. In other words, it is yet another "Light Riders" novel that will draw you in from page one and never let you go. This author deserves a blue ribbon for this series, because no matter how many she writes, they just keep beguiling and amazing book lovers everywhere."

Amy Lignor,
FEATHERED QUILL BOOK REVIEWS

The Time
Stealer

A Light Riders Novel

A Time Travel Mystery
by

Ann I. Goldfarb

TWO CATS PRESS
Sun City West, AZ

The Time Stealer

Copyright © 2014 Ann I. Goldfarb
Time Travel Mysteries

Cover design by Trevor Smith
(www.trevorsmithart.com)

All rights reserved. No part of this book, except the study guide, may be reproduced or transmitted in any form or by any means, electronic or mechanical, including photocopying, recording, or by an information storage retrieval system—with the exception of a reviewer, who may quote brief passages in a review to be printed in a newspaper or magazine or in a column or website via the internet—without written permission from the publisher.
Contact:
Two Cats Press, 13836 W. Terra Vista Dr.,
Sun City West, AZ 85375-5432

ISBN-13: 978-1-937083-42-7
ISBN-10: 193708342X
LCCN: 2014946479

This is a work of fiction. Names and characters are derived from the author's imagination. Any resemblance to people, living or deceased, is purely coincidental. Historical locations are intended to give this work of fiction a sense of authenticity and reality.

Visit the author's website:
www.timetravelmysteries.com

Printed in the U.S.A.

*In memory of Michaele McGrath,
whose incomparable sense of humor
inspired me to write this novel.
Her warmth and joyful spirit resonate
on each of these pages.*

Chapter One:

Aeden, Emerson College, Boston, Present Day

"Wait! Professor Heidecker! Wait!" I yelled as I stumbled down the steps from the theater arts building. He was making a beeline to the parking lot and either didn't hear me or chose not to. "WAIT!" I screamed again and this time everyone in the vicinity of Emerson's quad could hear me. The director of the theater department had no choice but to turn around and stand still while I raced towards him. Still trying to catch my breath, my words came out in spurts.

"Can't . . . do . . . this . . ."

"Take your time, Aeden," he mumbled. "What can't you do?"

"I can't cast your nephew in this play. I'm not good with children. Especially the ones in middle school. When I agreed to direct Children's Theater, it was supposed to be adults performing plays for kids, not kids on stage."

"Technically, yes, but this is an exception. I am going to be saddled with the little bugger for the next two months and it's the only way to keep him out of my hair, so find him a part in that play! I don't care if you cast him as a tree trunk, just cast him!"

"I don't understand. Shouldn't he be in school or something?"

"Oh, he should. He most definitely should. Trouble is, he's not. He's managed to accelerate and pass his finals two months before his eighth grade term at that ridiculous prep school ends."

"They can't just let him go for the rest of the year, can they?" My voice sounded more like a whine than a question.

"They can and they did. End of story. And while my sister and her husband go off somewhere in the Southwest to rekindle their marriage, I'm afraid I'm stuck with their only prodigy, Wendell Tyler Banton. So you see, Aeden, I have no choice and neither do you. You're a resourceful student, I'm sure you'll manage. I'll be bringing Wendell to your rehearsal tomorrow morning. Good day."

I stood on the sidewalk, mouth wide open, as Professor Heidecker approached the silver Audi sedan that looked as if it had just been polished. The other cars in the lot were still covered with dirty snow and grime, validating my observation that the man was the most exacting perfectionist I'd ever encountered. Too bad he was the head of the department and I was at his mercy. The only thing standing between me and my bachelor's degree was this final directing project. Nephew or not, I wasn't about to let some eighth grader undo four years of hard work. I kept muttering the kid's name under my breath as I walked back to the Greene Theatre where the cast, *my* cast, was rehearsing *Aladdin and the Wonderful Lamp.*

Wendell Tyler Banton. Wendell Tyler Banton. Who names their kid Wendell? Must be after a great grandfather or some other prestigious relative. The cast and crew had taken a five minute break the second Professor Heidecker marched towards the stage and motioned for me to stop everything and speak with him. His voice resonated throughout the theater and I could see the pained looks on everyone's face when he announced that the cast would now include his nephew. Before I had a chance to respond, he rushed out of the building with me only inches away from his expensive black Oxfords.

Our conversation near the front steps had not gone well and I needed to let the cast and crew know.

"I'm back," I shouted as I made my way to the stage. I grabbed my cup of coffee, now cold, from the table near the proscenium, took a quick gulp and spoke. "I'm sorry about this, guys. I'll need to do a quick re-write of the script tonight and find someplace to stick that kid."

"I can tell you where to stick him," someone shouted out and the place erupted in laughter.

"It can't be *that* bad, Aeden," came the reassuring voice of Ed Millington, my assistant director, and a junior majoring in stage and production management.

"Yes, yes it can. As if I didn't have enough to do. Look at me! I haven't even had time to get my hair done. The blond highlights are growing out and now I'm stuck babysitting some kid. I'll never get an appointment!"

Ed could see the panicked look on my face and I knew that wasn't good. I bit my lip, took a breath and continued.

"It'll be okay. We're troopers. We'll manage. Look, let's just do a quick run-through of Act II and tomorrow we can go over the revisions. We've got lots of time. Let's go! Places! Act II, Scene I."

"If you want, I can stop by and help you with the revisions," Ed whispered. I nodded and took another swallow of coffee. *Wendell Tyler Banton.* Even the name sounded like trouble. Of all the times to louse up something. It seems as if every year, no matter how carefully I plan it, something always goes wrong. The only bright spot was the fact that I'd have some control over the situation, unlike the other times in my past.

Back when I was twelve and my brother Ryn was thirteen, we were forced to clean out a hoarder's nest of a house that belonged to our great-great Auntie Zanne. That's when we discovered a box with prisms and formulas for time travel. Apparently, my aunt knew how to use Snell's Law of Refraction for manipulating time and space. Ryn couldn't leave it alone and as a result we wound up going back in time, unable to control anything. Fortunately, nature had a way of working things out. Too bad my brother didn't. Each year we somehow managed to wind up in a different place and time. And if that wasn't bad enough, his soon-to-be fiancée, Linna, figured out how to move horizontally and linearly in time. I took a deep breath. No matter how awful the situation was going to be with Wendell, at least it would be in the 21st century in Boston.

I leaned over to Ed and kept my voice low. "We can always make him a townsperson. The script has lots of those but I get the feeling that we'd better give him enough lines to keep him busy. I just have a bad, bad feeling about this."

Chapter Two:

Aeden

Wendell Tyler Banton arrived on stage the next day at precisely 8:42 a.m. Literally, on stage! Apparently he and his uncle were having some sort of squabble and the professor actually shoved him onto the stage and directly in front of the actors.

"You can't make me!" the kid screamed.

"I can. I will. And I just did. Have a good day, Wendell. I'll be back at 1:00 to pick you up."

Then, the professor peered into the darkened theatre where I was seated in the front row and announced, "If you need anything, Aeden, call the department secretary." Before I had a chance to respond, he exited past the curtains and out the back stage door. I stood up and shouted, "Take five, everyone!" and then quickly added, " NOT you, Wendell. Stay right where you are!"

Taking a deep breath, I raced up the stairs on stage right and approached Wendell before he decided to dart off somewhere.

"Hi Wendell. I'm Aeden, the director of this play. As you can see, we will be performing *Aladdin and the Wonderful Lamp*. We're pleased you can be part of the cast." I started to hand him a copy of the script but he brushed it aside.

"Look, lady, it's not Wendell. It's Dell. Dell T. You can call me Dell T."

I'm not one for glaring, but in this case, I made an exception.

"I'm not calling you Dell T. You're not a rapper. You're an eighth grader. But OK, Dell it is. And you can call me Director Aeden or Miss Aeden. Nothing else. Got it?"

The kid shrugged as I shoved the script into his hand. *Not too bad, Aeden, considering you didn't take a child psych course.*

"A paper script? You're handing me a paper script? I should at least get an iPad or something if I'm forced to be in this lousy play."

I tried to remain calm but Wendell—Dell, whatever-his-name-was, had just hit a nerve and it wasn't even 9:00 a.m. My eyes were still puffy and droopy from me being up most of the night to revise the script.

"No one gets an iPad for the script, Dell," I said. "It's much easier to use these pocket size scripts for writing cues and information until you learn the lines."

"You've got one," he replied as he pointed to the small desk in front of the stage.

"I need that for all sorts of applications, not just the script, oh my God, why am I telling you this? Look, just take a seat in the audience and watch the rehearsal. You'll be playing the part of Farzin, the sultan's advisor."

"I've seen Aladdin a zillion times on TV and there was no Farzin. No sultan's advisor."

I felt like smacking him over the head with the script and yelling, "That's because I had to write it into the script thanks to your uncle" but instead I kept my composure and replied, "Stage plays are adaptable and that's what we've done. Now, take a seat in the audience and watch the rehearsal. When your character appears on stage, I will walk you through the blocking. You do know what blocking is, don't you?"

"Yeah, I know. I've been in plays before."

"Good. Then we can get started."

Wendell darted ahead of me and plopped himself into a seat in the mid-section of the theater as I returned to my desk and called out, "Places everyone!"

It was a grueling rehearsal. Absolutely painful. At one point I even found myself muttering, "I could have been a museum curator . . . ." By noon we were all exhausted but no one threatened to quit. Not yet.

Wendell was quick to pick-up the blocking as well as his lines. He was also quick to criticize and question everything.

"What's my motivation for this line?"

"You don't need any motivation to announce 'the magician is here to see you.' Just say the line!" I could feel the heat rising in my face and was relieved when it was finally 1:00 p.m. and the kid's uncle returned to get him. Gauging from the looks on everyone else's faces, they were thankful as well.

"Same time tomorrow guys," I said as I started to click off my iPad. Funny, but it wasn't on the same page as before. I figured that Ed must have been checking something while I was showing the blocking to Wendell. I put it into my bag, grabbed the second cup of cold coffee from the table and headed up the aisle to the front doors of the building. The cast couldn't bolt out of there fast enough.

The tech crew had already turned off the house lights by the time I opened the auditorium door. My feet were lead and my head was throbbing. The five minute walk to the bus stop felt like fifty. When I finally trudged up the stairs to my apartment, I was too exhausted to think.

I microwaved an egg with some bacon bits and washed it down with peppermint tea. Went through my snail mail, reviewed the script notes, and watched repeats of "Castle" and "Modern Family" before calling it a night.

When the theme for "The Munsters" went off at 6:02 a.m., I sat up and looked around for my cell phone. I was still comatose when I answered it.

"Hullo?"

"Is this Aeden from the theater department? I hope my husband left me the right number."

"Yes, I'm---"

"This is Eleanor Heidecker, Wendell's aunt. Is he with you? Is he at the theater?"

"What? With me, no. I'm home. Rehearsal doesn't start for three hours."

"Well, he's missing. I can't bother my husband about it because he left last night for a symposium in New York. It's just like Wendell to do something like this. He's so unpredictable."

I cleared my throat and wiped my eyes.

"Maybe your nephew is with friends. Kids do that kind of thing."

"Wendell doesn't have any friends in Boston. And he couldn't have gone back to his home in Connecticut; he doesn't have any money or means to do that. I could just strangle him . . . unless somebody else has already . . . oh my God."

"Look, I'm sure he's fine. He's probably taking a walk in the neighborhood or something.

I'll get dressed and head over to the theater, Mrs. Heidecker. If he's there, I'll call you immediately."

"That kid is too smart for his own good. No wonder they let him finish the term early. They were too scared to see what else he'd do."

I felt my voice starting to crack.

"Else? What did he do?"

"My husband didn't tell you?"

"No, I'm afraid he didn't."

"As I said, Wendell is very talented. Junior boxing league, chess club . . . Did you know that he can translate Latin and Greek? Taught himself the classics. Imagine that!"

"Um . . . yes, but you said something about the school."

"Oh. *That.* The classics aren't the only thing that my nephew has succeeded in mastering. He's what you call a hacker. He can break into any computer system and that's what he did at his prep school. They're still trying to repair the damage."

I glanced at the kitchen table where I placed my iPad and took a deep breath.

"Did he change the grades? Is that why they ended his term early?"

"Oh, dear. If only it were that simple. No, Wendell got into the personnel files and altered the teacher evaluations."

"Oh my gosh."

"That's not all. The most damage occurred when he got into accounting and payroll."

By now I had walked over to my iPad and turned it on. Within seconds, I knew that whatever destruction that kid wrecked on his school, it was nothing compared to the havoc he was about to create.

"I've got to go, Mrs. Heidecker. I'll call you if he turns up."

I tapped the delete button and took a closer look at my iPad. Wendell Tyler Banton was not about to turn up anywhere in Boston. Or in this century, for that matter.

Chapter Three:

Aeden

My heart started to race and for a second I was almost lightheaded. Sinking into the couch with the iPad in my hand, I began to assess the damage. Obviously that kid had gotten his hands on my tablet sometime during the rehearsal. I mean, it wasn't as if I was sitting in front of the stage all the time. Not to mention the fact that Wendell wasn't in all of the scenes.

It didn't matter. He was able to break through the encryption and find the formulas for time travel. I never told my brother that I had copied them onto the iPad but I figured it was safer than just having them stored in an old cardboard box. Safer, maybe. Stupider? Yes. I even added Linna's discovery of linear transport to Snell's Laws of Refraction. So God knows where the boy could wind up.

Of all the possible nightmares in my life, this was the worst so far. I had to find that kid. My graduation depended on it. And technically, it was my fault for being so careless. *Give yourself a break, Aeden. How on earth were you supposed to know that Wendell Tyler Banton could probably hack into the national security database?*

I stood up, walked to the sink, splashed some water on my face and threw on some clothes. Then, I sat back down and took a closer look at the iPad. Computer genius or not, little Dell didn't bother to erase his browsing history. I had a fighting chance of finding out where he went.

Terrific. His first search was under lost civilizations. I cringed, picturing myself being strangled by a giant anaconda in the Amazon while Wendell looked for some missing Indian tribes. I kept going, hoping his search pattern would narrow. The good news was—it did. The bad news, and I mean *really* bad, was that it narrowed on Atlantis. Atlantis! The lost continent. Sure, why pick some missing tribe when you can search for a whole continent! Darn that kid!

By now my fingers were shaking. I had to put down the iPad and make myself a cup of tea. I didn't dare try coffee. After a few deep breaths, I continued to follow the websites he had explored. Yep, he was after Atlantis all right. Of all the idiotic things! Then again, I was dealing with a fourteen year-old, so in his mind it made perfect sense. I felt like grabbing him by the shoulders and screaming, "There is no Atlantis! You're going to find yourself somewhere in Ancient Greece!"

Calm down, Aeden and get a grip. Not Ancient Greece. Think back to your literature classes. If he's looking for Atlantis, he'd find himself immersed in another ancient culture— the Minoans.

By now I almost gagged. *When* did he decide to drop in on the Ancient Minoans? 2300 B.C.? 1600 B.C.? 1500 . . . This was a catastrophe. The Minoan civilization, if my memory was still intact, occupied Crete and Thera. Then a cataclysmic volcanic eruption was said to have wiped out Thera. Wasn't that something Plato wrote? My mind was spinning as I kept checking Wendell's browsing history.

The name Santorini popped up. It was a Greek island in the Aegean Sea known for its tourism and the myth that surrounded it. Ryn and Linna had talked about spending their honeymoon on Santorini a few years from now. I doubted very much that they would have wanted to get an early start. Especially one that involved Wendell Tyler Banton.

Santorini was said to be the shell of what was once Atlantis. That myth kept the tourism business going strong. I kept looking at the websites. *How much time did this kid spend with my iPad and what the heck was I doing?* Then, I remembered. I checked in on the costume department and spent some time with the prop master.

One thing became clear. Wendell had selected the island of Thera. It was the *when* that I was still struggling with.

I had no choice. I had to call Mrs. Heidecker back to see if her nephew had left any clues in his room. She was still frantic and out of breath when she picked up the phone.

"Aeden? Have you found him? Have you heard anything? Are you at the theater?"

"No and no. It's only been a few minutes since we've spoken, Mrs. Heidecker. I haven't left for the theater yet. I called you because I wondered if maybe your nephew left any phone numbers or information in his room that might give us a hint as to his whereabouts."

"No, absolutely nothing. Like I said before, he doesn't have any friends in Boston. The only thing he wrote down and left on his desk was a note about a video game. At least it appears that way. His handwriting is a mess."

"What did it say?"

"The letters are garbled but it looks like *Atari1750.* That's a video game of sorts, isn't it?"

Atari? Who plays Pong anymore? That was like way back in the seventies. I repeated the name over and over in my mind. Garbled letters.

Atari. Atari. He wasn't writing Atari. There was no Atari1750. He was writing Akrotiri! Akrotiri in 1750 B.C. Bingo! I've got it!

"Don't worry, Mrs. Heidecker. I'm on my way to the theater. I'll let you know if anything turns up. I'm sure he's just taking a walk or something."

You're such a liar, Aeden. I could hear my conscience getting the better of me. But honestly, what could I have said? *Your nephew stole some time travel formulas and right about now he's traipsing around in the 18th century B.C.?*

I immediately texted Ed Millington, told him I had a stomach bug and asked him to conduct the rehearsal. *Second lie in two minutes. Good going, Aeden.*

Then, I printed out the formulas from my iPad, opened the dresser drawer and took out a few small prisms that were hidden under my scarves. No time to lose. Wendell may have slipped back just a few minutes ago in our time but who knows how many hours, days or weeks he's been in the Bronze Age.

More than anything I wanted to call my brother, confess to what I did, and beg him to go back in time with me. He would have done it, moaning and groaning the entire time. I knew it wouldn't be fair. He was completing his graduate work at Stanford, not too far away from Linna's grad school. No, this was all on me. I tried not to think about all the things that could go wrong as I raced to the campus.

My fingers were trembling as I unlocked the door to Greene Theater and made my way to the costume department. We'd produced enough Greek tragedies for me to find something that I thought would blend into the Ancient Minoan culture. Anything would be better than jeans and a Boston Bruins T-shirt.

I stuffed my street clothes into a bag and headed to the stage. My cell phone and iPad were in my apartment along with my I.D. and credit cards. The Minoans didn't take Visa. For a brief second I wondered how Wendell managed to do this, but like his aunt said, he was an extremely intelligent boy. Intelligent enough to figure out how to go back in time.

Chapter Four:

Aeden

It had to be done indoors. Too early for sunlight and not enough of it. Too many cloudy days in March. With my clothes folded up into a nondescript canvas bag, I took the steep staircase to the catwalk and turned on the biggest ellipsoidal spotlight I could find. Then, I centered it so that the beam would be directly in front of the stage.

By the time I had reviewed my notes and placed the prisms appropriately, I glanced at the wall clock in the rear of the auditorium. *7:48 a.m.* I had less than thirty minutes before Ed Millington would be unlocking the door and freaking out that someone left such an expensive light on all night long.

I knew how the time component worked but adjusting for travel linearly was new to me. It was something Linna had figured out. One slight miscalculation and I could wind up in the right century but the wrong place. I shuddered to think about it. *Fish or cut bait, Aeden. You don't have all day.* I swear it was as if Ryn was standing right behind me.

As I stood a few feet back from the center of the stage, I checked the beams against the prisms. The small paper protractor that I kept in my bag was starting to show its wear. Still, it was functional and a heck of a lot better than having to use trigonometry to figure out the angles. Taking a deep breath, I glanced at the clock and stepped inside the circle. *8:07 a.m.* That was the last image I remembered seeing before blacking out.

Each time it's different and each time it's scary as hell. The pounding in the back of my head, at first slow and rhythmic, became wild and disjointed until it finally dissipated. A soft, lapping sound replaced the heavy hammering. I knew my body was there but I couldn't feel anything. Like every other time, I kept my eyes closed, too frightened of what I might actually see.

My toes were the first part of me to regain any feeling. They felt damp and stuck to the soles of the sandals that I had swiped from the costume room. I was standing upright, something that's never happened before. And there was warmth, the kind you get from the summer sun. I reached to my shoulder and could feel the strap from the canvas bag. *OK, Aeden, time to open your eyes.*

Too scared to stare straight ahead, I looked down. My feet were sinking slightly into wet sand. Bloody sand. *Oh my God! Was I bleeding so badly that the sand had absorbed it?* Jolted by fear, I opened my eyes wide and scanned the entire beach. All of the sand was red. It wasn't me. It was this place. Red sand and deep marine blue water. In front of me the sea was endless. Behind me, tall red cliffs framed the horizon. Judging from the position of the sun, it had to be afternoon.

The water lapped my toes and I wasn't sure if the tide was coming in or going out. I stepped back and sank into the soft crimson ground, too exhausted and too exhilarated to grasp the one glaring mistake I had made—I had no way to communicate with anyone. By the time I realized it, it was too late. Someone was walking towards me.

I stood up, brushed the sand off of me and took a breath as a man about my age approached. Tall, sandy brown hair, wearing a tunic with ornate red, gold and blue trim. A large bronze medal fastened to the white linen glimmered in the sunlight. Not a slave. They wouldn't wear such fancy clothing. I nodded, expecting him to say something but he kept walking as if I wasn't there. I turned my head and watched as he made his way down the beach. Suddenly, I remembered something Linna had told me about traveling linearly in time.

"It's like fan blades, Aeden. When they move so fast no one can see them. It takes a while for time to slow down. Until then, the traveler is invisible."

"So that's what it was," I thought to myself as I took a closer look at the sea and the red sand. "No one can see me. Not yet." Off in the distance a crescent shaped ship was making its way towards the shore. Odd that its sail looked as if it was floating on top of a canopy. As it got closer I could see its colors—red, gold and blue, the same colors in that man's tunic. It couldn't be a coincidence. By now it was in full view with at least twenty oars on each side of the ship.

A sudden splash of water and all movement stopped. The oars were lifted and something was happening. More splashing, this time with higher waves hitting the vessel. I could hear the men yelling but couldn't understand them. The water scattered violently near the front of the ship and a team of men started to toss netting into the water. I laughed. They were fishing and the catch must have been a big one.

Turning away from the water, I took another look at the large red rock formations along the shore. They seemed to have crevices and openings. Caves perhaps? I made a mental note to avoid them at all costs. After my last experience underground in Missouri, caves were the last place I wanted to be. Unfortunately, it didn't work out that way. Within seconds, a procession of people approached and this time they saw me.

Chapter Five:

Aeden

Pallbearers. That's what they were. Pallbearers. It was a long procession of a half dozen men in front, followed by the chosen four who carried a body for burial. Behind them were three or four women in fancy tunics, followed by four or five more ladies in simple linen smocks like the one I had taken from the costume department. By the time I realized what type of costume I had snatched, it was too late.

One of the fancy dressed women grabbed me by the elbow and yanked me to the back of the procession. I didn't need a translator to figure out what was going on. Apparently she thought I was one of the house slaves who had gotten out of the line. I couldn't very well make a run for it so I followed along as if this was exactly what I had planned to do for the day. I could almost hear my brother laughing. *Good going, Aeden. You couldn't have picked out a tunic belonging to a royal family?*

The procession moved steadily down the beach and then started to veer off towards the red rocks. *Oh no. Don't tell me they're going to bury this guy in a cave?* They were. We slipped into the narrow opening and ducked down so that we wouldn't be slammed into the rock ceiling that framed the opening. The smell of candle wax and oil permeated the place. Inside, someone was playing the lyre. Soft, eerie tones echoed in the small cavern. I stood back with the others and watched as the body was lowered into the ground.

A man with a long yellow robe said a few words and the ladies in the procession began to sob. By now my eyes had gotten used to the semi-darkness and I could see a few narrow passageways that probably led to more burial chambers. I figured that we would be here for a few more minutes and then head back to wherever this family resided. Again, I was wrong. Apparently burying someone was an overnight vigil. At that moment I just wanted to get my hands on Wendell's neck and wring it!

Someone poked me in the elbow and motioned for me to take a long clay vessel from them. I watched carefully. It was wine and I was the server. Terrific. *Just act as if it's a part in a play, Aeden, and you'll be OK.* Along with the other slaves, we served wine to the ladies and some sort of dried fruits. The men of the household had their own slaves who catered to them.

For hours I sat on the cold stone floor listening to women wail and sob while the man with the yellow tunic threw some sort of aromatic leaves into a fire pit. The cave smelled as if a hundred tubes of analgesic heat rub had been opened. *At least your sinuses won't get clogged up, Aeden.*

My muscles ached and my eyes burned. I thought the night would never end. At daybreak, the procession exited the cave and made its way back down the beach. Off in the distance, the same fishing vessel was sailing towards the shore. I could have sworn I heard Wendell's voice but I knew it was the combination of imagination and lack of sleep. There was no one on the beach except our procession and unfortunately, Wendell Tyler Banton was not part of it.

Chapter Six:

Wendell

Argh! I landed in water. Water of all things! She didn't have *that* in her notes. At least it wasn't freezing. I had to lose my sneakers in order to swim to the surface and when I did— BAM! I was trapped in some sort of netting. I kicked. I wrestled. I screamed. But I was stuck. Suddenly, I was suspended in air. Caught in a net as if I was some sort of fish. I tried to turn my head but couldn't see what was behind me.

Three or four hands grabbed me through the netting and tossed me onto the hard wooden surface of a ship. My khaki shorts and faded shirt had gotten so ripped up that they practically fell off of me. I was covered in sticky sand and scales. Probably what was left in the fish net. Gross. The only good news was that I had done it. Used her formulas to travel through time. The calculations were easy and the Hollywood light bulbs in Aunt Eleanor's guest bathroom were perfect.

I started to smile until I looked around. I should have arrived in Atlantis, but something was wrong. The ship looked too primitive—linen sails with colorful drawings of dolphins jumping through waves, and lots of men holding wooden oars. *Thanks a whole heck of a lot Miss Aeden for screwing this up for me!*

I could see the beach and red rocks in the distance. Someone was sitting on the sand but I couldn't tell if it was a man or a woman. We were too far out. Before I had a chance to get a better look, a tall guy with a long braid in the middle of his bald head walked towards me and spoke. He had to be the captain. He was the only one wearing something other than a loincloth.

"Συναποκαλέω."

My name. The guy wanted to know my name. All I could do was stare at him and swallow the salty seawater that had gotten into my mouth. He said it again. A word I recognized. Sort of. It was Greek. Ancient Greek. *Holy Crap! I landed in Ancient Greece. This stinks! I wanted to find Atlantis. Now I had to figure out how to get out of here.*

There was no Greek word for Dell so I just mumbled something. Next thing I knew he repeated the name "Didikase" and bowed his head. Within seconds, two bald men with smaller braids in the middle of their heads handed me a dry loincloth. Was I supposed to put it on in front of them?

They turned away and I quickly slipped into it like a two minute locker change for gym. Everyone seemed to be talking at once—the men seated by the oars, the men standing near the sails and the men surrounding the captain. From out of nowhere, another man approached me carrying a tray of small dried fish and fruit. He placed it in front of me and said something that sounded like "phago," the Greek word for eat. The fish was wrinkled and red. I knew I'd barf if I took a bite. I tried the fruit instead. Some sort of fig. At least I could keep that down.

Then, another guy showed up and shoved a two handled cup in front of me and waited for me to take a drink. It was sweet and fruity so I drank the entire thing. For a quick second, my face felt flushed and I knew what I had just swallowed— wine. I expected to get lightheaded but nothing happened. *They probably diluted the stuff to make it last longer.*

The guy filled the cup again and waited for my response. The last thing I remembered before waking up and staring at constellations that I didn't quite recognize was that the second cup of wine tasted different from the first.

My elbows kept hitting against the sides of the ship. I knew I was crammed into the back since I could feel the wood with both of my hands. Someone had tossed a blanket over me. At least they didn't want me to freeze my tail off. No one was moving. No one was awake. The boat kept rocking back and forth in the darkness. If it wasn't for the fact that someone had lit one hell of a bonfire in the distance, it would have been impossible to figure out where the shore was.

I had to wait it out. It would be too stupid to jump into the sea and swim to shore. They'd have to anchor soon enough. I mean, there was no way to hang on to a bunch of dead fish for days on end without having them rot. If I could get to the beach, I'd look for some glass and the right angle of the sun to get the heck out of here. Maybe I was imagining it, but I had the creepy feeling that I was in trouble. I mean, who gives a kid a knock-out drug with his wine? Then again, maybe they thought I'd go berserk on their boat and didn't want to deal with it. Nah, I was in trouble. I just didn't know what kind.

Chapter Seven:

Wendell

I squinted as the sunlight hit my eyes. Everyone was up already and fishing. Big smelly grey fish were tossed onto the deck and flopped around. The men grabbed them, speared them and hung them out over the edges of the boat. No one asked me to help and that was just as well. I watched as men tossed the nets and pulled in the squirmy grey fish. I swore I'd never open another can of tuna again.

Someone offered me a drink but I refused. *You don't think you're going to try the same thing again, do you?* I stayed out of the way and waited. By the time the sun was midway up in the sky, the ship headed to shore. Lots of red cliffs and the peaks of volcanoes in the distance. Yep, we were headed to some Grecian island. If it was Thera, then I was in the right place, just the wrong time.

I could see a long line of people walking down the beach. No one was running. No one was playing. Talk about creepy. I leaned over the edge of the boat to get a better look when all of sudden, I got hit by a stinking fish that one of the men intended to toss onto the deck. It bounced off of me first and I screamed.

That apparently set off the whole ship and they started laughing. I kept quiet for the rest of the afternoon, and with the exception of eating a few more pieces of dried fruit, I didn't have much interaction with anyone. This wasn't exactly a fun-filled fishing charter. By late afternoon we made it to shore. It was a city, all right, but definitely not Atlantis. *Couldn't that girl at least have gotten her time travel formulas right?*

At least twenty wooden docks and crowds of people were waiting for boats to come in. Vendors selling all sorts of fish that had been drying out in the sun. At first I thought it was just a fish market but the closer we got, the more I realized that this was the mega-market for Ancient Greek shopping. I could see stalls with clothing, pottery and food. And the crowd looked worse than Costco's during Thanksgiving.

At least I fit in with my white loincloth. I just hoped no one intended to shave my head. I didn't need to blend in that much. The women and girls were wearing ankle length tunics, mostly white with some blue edges. A few men had tunics as well in the same red, gold and blue colors like the one the ship captain was wearing. Must be the royalty.

As the fishermen started to tie the boat to the dock, I moved forward so that I could make a jump and run for it, even though I was barefoot.

"Ohxi" someone yelled just as one of the men grabbed me by the shoulder. A quick shove and my butt landed on one of the worn wooden benches by the oars. It was so smooth that I practically slipped off of it. Okay, so maybe I shouldn't have tried to get the heck out of there so fast, but geez, it wasn't as if I was a criminal or anything.

The same guy motioned to one of the other fishermen, and the next thing I knew, that guy made a mad dash off the boat, across the marketplace and down one of the narrow streets. My new-found bodyguard kept an eye on me while the other crew members unloaded the fish. About twenty minutes later, the mad-dash-for-the-street guy came running back, this time with four men who were all decked out in the fancier tunics. He took one look at me, shouted something to the bodyguard guy and watched while I got pushed off of the boat and onto the deck. *If this is their official welcoming committee, I really don't want to hang out and meet the rest of the city. Just need to find some glass or a mirror and get the hell out of here.*

As I stumbled forward, the men stepped back and took a closer look at me. One of them pointed to my feet and immediately took off for the marketplace. The others whispered quietly to each other while I just stood there like some sort of carnival attraction. I didn't have to stand long. The guy returned and handed me a new pair of sandals that he must have gotten from one of the vendors. Maybe this wasn't going to be too bad after all. Still, I had a lousy feeling about it and didn't plan on staying long.

Once the sandals were on my feet, the four men directed me to walk with them. Not that I had much choice. The bodyguard guy was giving me menacing looks and a small crowd had gathered around us. Other than the fact that I still had my hair, I didn't look a whole lot different from them. And it wasn't as if I was wearing my clothes. That might have freaked them out. It had to be something else.

We walked past the vendors, through the marketplace and down one of the winding streets. The crowd surrounding us had gotten bigger—men, women, women holding babies, and kids my age. The girls had long curly hair and dangling earrings. They gasped, giggled and stared. Terrific. Just like a dance at my old prep school. Then, a few of them reached out to touch me. *What the heck? Cut it out!*

Whitewashed houses that looked like small apartment buildings were on either side of the street. Most of them had walls in front with paintings of fish, birds, and bulls, just like the ones I saw on the boat. We kept walking and no one said anything. A few more people came out of their houses and tried to touch me, too. It started to make my flesh crawl. More walking. This time, uphill. The street got wider and there were fewer houses. In the distance I could see the greyish volcanoes.

Straight ahead was a huge house. At first I thought it was a mansion but when I saw this huge muscular guy guarding the door, I figured it was probably a temple or maybe even a palace. I never got the chance to find out. I only made it as far as the courtyard before two small chunky men came out of nowhere and dragged me off. I didn't go quietly.

Chapter Eight:

Wendell

"**A**físte me ísiho!" It meant "Leave me alone!" I screamed it at least five times but they ignored me. In fact, one of them even tried to cover my mouth. Next thing I knew I was looking at a small rectangular pool with columns and bushes all around it. *Great. For the second time since I got here, I'm going to wind up underwater.*

One of the men pointed to my loincloth and sandals, motioning for me to take them off. *Over your dead body, buddy. I'm not stripping down in front of two complete strangers. I don't care if this is the official welcome to wherever the heck I am!*

It was ugly. I fought. I kicked and I tried to run. They were faster and stronger. I was underwater and naked before I knew it. *Freaking nightmare. Even a fraternity hazing wouldn't take it that far.* At least they didn't go in with me. A third chunky guy arrived a few minutes later with a large white towel in his hand. *Don't you even think of it!*

I can dry myself! I snatched it from his hand and immediately started to dry myself off. He leaned over to rub some sort of scented oil on me.

What's with these people? Do you have to pass a smell test before they let you inside? I backed away and yelled "Afíste me ísiho!" again. This time it worked. They stepped back and let me put on a new loincloth and a white tunic. One of them motioned to an archway and we walked through it past a large courtyard that had more paintings of dolphins and waves on the walls. I could hear voices echoing around me but no one was in sight except for my new-found escorts.

They led me into a small room filled with platters of fruit, dried fish, tomatoes, olives and flat bread. Bowls of oil and honey were everywhere along with flowers and plants. Vases of water and wine, too. It reminded me of those rooms during calling hours but there were no dead bodies. I could see a cot in the corner and a large pot on the floor. So much for their toilet facilities. The only windows were near the ceiling. Enough to let in the light, but not the view. No way to escape either. I couldn't out run the guards but maybe I could hurl something at them and get the heck out of there.

The dead fish were too small and I'd need an arsenal of olives. I grabbed three of the biggest tomatoes I could find and wound up my backhand pitch better than Nolan Ryan. Got two of the guys in the face and the other in the chest. Got as far as the courtyard before running straight into a colossal bruiser who made my bodyguards look like the Lollipop Guild.

I was back in my "guest quarters," this time with a solid wooden door bolted from the other side.

"Voíthia!" I screamed for help as loud as I could. Finally gave up and ate a few olives before lying down on the cot and closing my eyes. What a stupid mess-up. I should be in Atlantis by now, watching the orbs of light in the circular canals, or maybe even finding the gold horsemen in the Temple of Poseidon. And the ships . . . they'd be full of technology that we'd never heard of. Not crescent shaped fishing trawlers. I blame this all on Aeden. She couldn't even get a math formula right. Because of her, I'm stuck in this room waiting for someone to unbolt the door.

I'd have to be faster next time around. If there was a next time. I watched as the sunlight slowly disappeared from the windows. Ate the bread and drank the water. *Yeah, no way I'd drink the wine again.* Dusk. Dusk and not even a candle. Outside I could hear music playing. Some sort of string instrument. I screamed again. This time louder. "Voíthia!"

A voice yelled back. Something about the sea

and the gods. It took me a while but I figured it out and when I did, I wanted to kick myself for learning Ancient Greek.

Chapter Nine:

Aeden

The procession moved quietly down the beach. In the early morning light I could get a better look at my surroundings. Greyish black volcanoes stood behind the red cliffs like sentinels. They appeared to be dormant, but didn't everyone think that Mt. Vesuvius was dormant, too? I kept walking, taking the sea air into my lungs.

After what seemed like hours, I could see a city or village ahead of us. Towards the shore, ships were anchoring on an endless line of wooden docks and the place looked overrun with people. As we got nearer, I realized what I was staring at—a marketplace! Complete with vendors, food, clothing and everything in-between. Behind the center of the city were countless streets with rows of two and three story houses. I gasped when I got a better look at the walls. I'd never seen artwork like that anywhere—paintings of sea creatures, waves, fruits, and bulls, all done in primary colors.

Our procession skirted behind the vendors and headed uphill. As I turned around to look back, I could see some sort of hubbub near the docks. Lots of people. Lots of noise. I knew I'd have to find a way to make it back into the center of the city to look for Wendell but I couldn't very well leave my place in the line without some sort of recrimination. *It's your banner day, Aeden. You picked out the slave costume!*

The bottoms of my feet were getting blisters and I called Wendell all sorts of names under my breath. None of them came close to what I was really thinking. Our procession twisted and turned through so many winding streets that I was getting dizzy. At last we reached a huge house set back from the street. Olive trees and small bushes surrounded it. The walls had the same designs as the others with one exception—a huge red and white bull that appeared to be tossing a man over its horns. I shuddered and kept moving.

The guard at the large wooden doors stared straight through us as we entered. The front of the procession turned to the right of the courtyard and those of us in the rear moved to a large kitchen area to the left. A middle aged woman with her hair piled high on her head pointed to baskets of fruit and handed me some sort of a knife. At least I wasn't told to wash any pots. Ryn would have been beside himself laughing. *"Hey, Aeden, you got yourself into the pot scrubbing deal in Morenci, not me."* He would conveniently forget about the fact that he told the kitchen help from the 1952 Summer Theater Playhouse in Missouri that I enjoyed scouring pots and pans. So why was it that whenever I went back in time, I wound up doing kitchen duty?

I took the knife and started peeling the fruits that looked as if they needed it. Everyone in that kitchen was cutting, peeling or placing things on platters. I could smell some sort of bread from ovens in another kitchen. Glad I didn't get stuck there. It was afternoon when we were finally done and someone directed me and another slave to take the platters across the courtyard. When no one was looking, I hid the knife in a corner of the kitchen. I don't know why, but I had the strangest feeling that I would need it.

As we crossed the courtyard I could hear the sound of splashing water. Probably one of the family members enjoying a swim or a bath. *Next time, be a little bit more particular about the costumes you pick out, Aeden.* We entered a small room with a cot and some sort of chamber pot. The other slave and I placed the platters on the round tables before being ushered out by one of the guards. Whoever got here before us filled the room with so many flowers that I started to sneeze. The other slave spat on the floor and said something to me but all I could do was nod.

For the next hour or so we swept the kitchen floor and took turns taking the discarded fruit and vegetables to a compost area just a few yards away. When no one was looking, I shoved pieces of the unwanted food into my mouth. It was nearly dusk when I found myself serving trays of food to a room full of men who kept holding out their cups for more wine. The women had to wait until the men had finished eating before they could be served. When the last platter was returned to the kitchen, I all but collapsed. I staggered behind the other female house slaves and fell into a small cot on the floor of the room we shared. No one said anything to me. They didn't have to. Slaves came and went. Bought and sold. Served and died. By now I really wanted to strangle Wendell.

Sleep came fast. The sound of someone screaming woke me for a second but I wasn't sure if I actually heard anything or if I had just dreamt it. By the time I learned the truth, it was too late.

Chapter Ten:

Aeden

I knew that I had to get the heck out of that place and back to the center of the city in order to find Wendell. The only way was for me to sneak out before sunrise. Thankfully, that scream woke me up while it was still dark. I slipped quietly from my cot and walked slowly toward the archway that led to the courtyard.

Small oil lamps on the walls of the courtyard cast eerie shadows against the walls. I kept walking. I had to remember where the kitchen was and where I had stashed that knife. The hallways seemed longer than they did before. The semi-darkness was throwing me off and every little creak or noise gave me the chills. I kept moving, too scared to stop. My eyes darted from wall to wall looking for the archway that led into the kitchen.

The smell of a fire pit hit my nostrils. I had found the kitchen and raced towards it, unaware that my sandals were making a thudding noise against the tile floor. No sooner did I step inside when I felt a large hand on my shoulder. I turned my head around and faced one of the guards.

" 'Sko'pile." It was a command. Something he wanted me to do. Wordless, I took a deep breath and swallowed. He pointed to the woven baskets on the floor that were filled with herbs but I still didn't understand. I started to walk towards them when a noise in the courtyard got the guard's attention and he turned away. In that split second I ran through the kitchen looking for the spot where I had hidden the knife. My fingers had no sooner grasped its metal blade when the guard returned with another slave. I let out a slow breath. He didn't see what I had done. The other slave looked to be about my age. She nodded to me and immediately picked up one of the baskets. I wasted no time doing the same thing, hiding the knife underneath the dried herbs. As we walked back into the courtyard, she whispered three words to me. Two of them sounded familiar— gods and sea. I had studied enough Ancient Greek tragedies to recognize them. The Minoan language had to be pretty darn close. *Start making the connections, Aeden. You'll need them.* I shook my head and we kept walking.

The front doors were unbolted and the two of us stepped outside with the baskets of herbs. It was still dark. How long before sunrise? I had no idea. The walkway was illuminated with small oil lamps that stretched as far as I could see. We didn't take the same path that brought me here yesterday. Instead, we walked to the side of the house and followed an up-hill trail towards the volcanoes. Even with the oil lamps, I kept losing my footing, tripping over small rocks and ruts. The girl, on the other hand, seemed to know this path quite well. I imagined we were going to some spot for a ceremony or something of the kind.

The sky was starting to lighten towards the horizon. It wouldn't be too long before sunrise. I'd have to think quickly to get out of there and race downhill towards the city. I knew if I made a run for it, she'd scream and the guards would be all over me. I had to bide my time. *Bide your time? Are you nuts, Aeden? And by the way, who in their right mind uses the word "bide?" Create a damn diversion and get the hell out of there!*

I swear it was as if my brother was talking to me. Too little sleep and not enough food was wreaking havoc with my mind. The slope was getting steeper and my legs were starting to cramp up. A few yards ahead I could see a rock staircase that curved around a bend in the hill. There were fewer oil lamps and they weren't as bright. The steps got narrower and taller as we made our way to a flat clearing. By now the sky was turning a hazy pink. The sun would be up in minutes. I could see a huge flat stone held up by four boulders. Two large oil lamps illuminated the area. *They're not coming here for a picnic, Aeden. You know what this is.*

The girl started to place the aromatic herbs around the flat stone and motioned for me to do the same. She repeated the same three words —gods, sea and that other word that I couldn't comprehend. *Thusia.* I didn't need to understand it. Suddenly, it all made sense. We were preparing the place for a sacrifice and I had the sickening feeling that it wasn't going to be an animal.

Chapter Eleven:

Wendell

The music outside my windows was getting on my nerves. If that wasn't bad enough, some sort of chanting began and it wouldn't stop. I never slept a wink. On and on, wailing, chanting, and wailing. *Hey, I'm the freaking one you're going to kill so why are you guys so upset?*

I tried screaming for help but I was wasting my breath. I figured that when they opened the door to this room in the morning, I'd give one of them a kick in the shins and get out of there. Turned out it was impossible. Not the kick. I tried it as soon as the door was unbolted. I couldn't even reach the guy's shin! Linebackers weren't that big.

Both of those stinking bruisers held me while some old lady poured water on my feet and dripped oil on my head. It was pitch black outside but that didn't stop them from dragging me up a hill. The worst part was that they took the musicians with them.

I didn't go quietly. I yelled at the top of my lungs and refused to walk. It didn't matter. They dragged my butt anyway. It was getting light out and I could see two slave girls further up on the path. Like that was going to help. They were probably assigned to pouring more oil on my head. I kept screaming.

I bellowed and yowled until we were face to face with them. That was the second I realized that everything was about to change.

Chapter Twelve:

Aeden

Burnt offerings. Human sacrifice. They were all part of ancient cultures. My stomach twisted into knots from the mere thought of it. *Please don't make me stay and watch. I couldn't bear it.* Was it going to happen right away? At dawn? I pointed to the slab of stone and repeated the same three words that the girl had said. Then, I looked up at the sky hoping she'd figure out that I was asking her *when*. *When* were they going to slaughter some innocent person?

She looked back at me, pointed upward and said "Helios." I knew the word! Sun! The sacrifice was going to take place at noon. I had no choice but to make sure that I wasn't going to witness it. Besides, I couldn't waste another minute. I had to be searching for Wendell. That kid probably got himself into a mess somewhere in this city and I'd be in a bigger one if I couldn't deliver him back to his aunt and uncle.

When the girl wasn't looking, I tucked the small knife into the shoulder straps of my tunic, grabbed the empty basket and waited for her to start down the hill. It was already dawn by the time we had reached the bottom of the steep stairs. Below us I could hear music. The same tune, but more melodic. More than one person was playing the lyre. Then, out of nowhere, I heard a blood curdling scream. Loud enough to send chills down my back. The music was getting louder and the scream was relentless.

The girl motioned for me to step back. By now the path was wide enough for a few people to pass by us. It had to be the guards bringing the sacrificial victim to his or her place of honor. I wanted desperately to close my eyes and not look, but I couldn't. My head turned to face the direction of the music and I could see three or four musicians approaching. They were followed by two enormous guards who were obviously dragging someone forward.

The girl and I stood motionless. She waited out of respect. I froze out of fear. The screams continued but there was something oddly familiar about them. I couldn't place it at first and when I did, I could swear my heart was in my throat.

Wendell! It was Wendell. Wendell Tyler Banton was their sacrificial victim. I was overcome with terror and anger. Not a great combination. *Serves you right for messing with my computer you little jerk! That's payback for you! But not today, kid. I'll find my own payback for you. If I can get you out of this . . .*

The musicians and the guards were just a few feet from us. *Stop screaming, Wendell, and look around you!* I stepped forward, close enough for him to see who I was.

"AEDEN!" His voice resonated around us and I quickly put a finger to my lips signaling for him to shut the heck up. He gave a quick nod before being dragged to the flat stone. The girl shook my elbow and waved for me to get moving. The ceremony wouldn't start for a few hours. There was still time for me to figure out something.

We were halfway down the hill when the girl motioned for us to step back from the path again. I looked behind me. The two large guards were making their way down the hill along with all of the musicians except one. I could hear the soft unsettling music in the background. One of the musicians had to remain to guard the "gift offering" and let the gods know that they would soon be appeased.

My mind was racing. I had to get to Wendell before the next procession arrived. Quickly, I stumbled forward, dropped my basket and pretended to strain my ankle. I winced, held my foot and forced my eyes to tear. To add to my dramatic performance, I tried taking a few steps before grabbing my ankle again. The girl said something to me and took off running. She'd be back with help. I held my breath until she was out of view and then I ran as fast as I could up the hill, up the steps and over to Wendell.

The musician, a slight, elderly man, stopped playing and looked up when I arrived. *Think of it like a scene in a play, Aeden. You can do it.* I stormed over to him as if he had committed the worst affront ever, grabbed the small string instrument from him and motioned for him to get down the hill. When he refused to move, I removed the knife from the band on my tunic and thrust it towards him. Aghast, he stepped away from me and ambled down the staircase. I didn't have much time. The girl would bump into the musician on her way back and she'd know what I had done.

For once, Wendell was speechless but it didn't last longer than a second or two.

"Good going, Aeden! Get me out of here!"

"Don't you 'Aeden' me, you spoiled little twerp! And it's 'Miss Aeden' to you."

"Fine, fine. Just untie me!"

"What an imbecilic, insane, inconsiderate, idiotic thing to do!"

"Can you think of any words that don't start with the letter *i?*"

"Oh, I can think of them all right, I just can't say them out loud!"

"You're not going to stand there and yell at me all day, are you? Come on, untie me! Get me out of here! You know what they've got planned for me!"

"I do. In fact, I was even thinking of helping them start the fire!"

"They're going to burn me? Is that what you think?"

"Burn you, clobber you over the head with a rock, plunge a knife in your chest . . . How am I supposed to know about human sacrifice? You picked a great time to time travel, Wendell."

"It's Dell. Dell T."

"Whatever. These are the Minoans and I have no idea what they have in mind, so yeah, we've got to get the blazes out of here and fast!"

No sooner did I finish my sentence when I could hear footsteps charging up the hill.

Chapter Thirteen:

Wendell

That giant Behemoth of a guard had tied my hands behind my head. Probably to a rock or something. Same deal with my feet. Aeden started slashing the rope apart behind me and I could feel the blade nick my skin.

"Hey, careful," I said. "You're going to cut me."

"I could do a lot worse. Quiet, Wen . . . Dell. We don't have much time."

She was fast. Cut through those bindings like she'd done it before. I stood up and looked down the hill. People were on their way up here. This time without the music. I turned towards her.

"So, now what? Got a plan?"

"Yeah, it's called *run for your life* and I mean it, Dell. Run!"

"Couldn't we time travel back? I still haven't found Atlantis."

"Atlantis? Atlantis? There is no Atlantis, you

moron. This is as sophisticated as it gets. Meet the Ancient Minoans—if they don't decide to sacrifice you first. Now hurry up!"

She pointed to a really narrow path above us and took off running. I bolted after her and didn't stop moving until my stomach started to cramp. By that time, we had gone so far up the hill that the volcanoes looked really close.

"Slow down, slow down. Do you think they're still behind us?"

"I don't hear them, Dell, but that doesn't mean a thing. Keep going."

"I'm going to collapse if we run any more. I need to rest."

"Rest? You want to rest? If we stop now you'll be resting on that nice, flat slab. Keep moving, Dell. I mean it."

The path was all but gone, only scrub brush and rocks. It didn't matter. We kept climbing. Finally, Aeden sat on the ground and waved me over to her.

"I think you're OK for a while, Dell."

"What makes you say that?"

"Look at where the sun is in the sky. It's past noon. I think they needed to make their sacrifice at noon. You're safe. At least for another day. Maybe longer if they don't catch us."

"We can still time travel back, can't we?"

"Not without glass or a mirror. And what

about the vibrations? Which, by the way, how *did* you do it?"

"The vibrations? The sound? I plugged in my uncle's electric shaver. Boy, is Aunt Eleanor going to be pissed when she finds it in her guest bathroom!"

I swore I saw her start to smile before she spoke again.

"We've got to get to a place that has the right elements for us. One that's as far away from here as we can get. We might as well keep climbing."

The ground beneath us changed color and there were no bushes or anything green for that matter. We had reached the base of one of the volcanoes.

"Shh, Dell. Do you hear that? Sounds like running water."

At first I thought Aeden might have been oxygen deprived but then I listened. She was right. I did hear moving water and lots of it.

"Hurry up, Dell, and follow the noise."

Instead of climbing, we started to traverse the volcano. The sound of gushing water got louder. I edged past her to get a better look and my foot slipped on the wet surface. Before I knew it, I was flat on my butt inches away from the highest waterfall I'd ever seen.

"Whoa! It goes straight down!"

Aeden looked over my shoulder and I could

hear her gasp.

"Straight down and out! Take a good look!"

It was amazing. The waterfall ran straight down between two of the volcanoes. Not only that but it formed some sort of river or channel that led right out to the ocean. We were on an island and we were looking at the other side.

Aeden's voice got really soft and slow.

"You know they're going to catch up with us if we keep climbing. Besides, we'll be exhausted when they do. Now's our chance, Dell. We jump into this waterfall and down to that channel."

Was she insane? Jump into the waterfall? That thing had to be at least two hundred feet tall. And what if the water below wasn't deep? We'd crush our skulls. I took another look and got dizzy.

"Couldn't we just climb faster? We'd outrun them."

"Is it because you don't know how to swim?"

I wasn't sure if she was being sarcastic like some adults get, or really concerned.

"Yeah, I can swim. But . . ."

"No reason to wait then, let's do it!"

She could see that I was hesitating and I could see that she was really, really serious. Enough to try and throw me over the edge. Some great choice. Get sacrificed to the gods or jump to my death. I took my chances and walked slowly to the lip edge just above the falls.

"NOW!" she yelled as she grabbed my wrist, leaned forward and used all the momentum she had to shove us off. It was only when I was a few feet away from the water that she let go. I think I went in feet first but I couldn't be sure. It happened so fast that I was underwater before I knew it. When I got to the surface Aeden was a few feet from me with the biggest grin I'd ever seen.

"Get used to this stuff, Dell, if you ever plan to time travel again."

I wasn't so sure. Behind her, I could see two giant fins moving towards us.

Chapter Fourteen:

Aeden

I could see the terror on his face. Good. I thought maybe it would teach him a lesson.

"You're OK. The water's not even cold."

"Sharks! Sharks!"

I spun my head around and tried to remain perfectly still. I could see two enormous fins moving straight towards us. *Try to stay calm, Aeden. Have you ever heard of sharks in the Aegean Sea?* There might not have been historical references to man-eating fish near Ancient Greece but I wasn't about to take a chance.

"Swim as fast as you can to the shore, Dell! Get moving!"

As I reached out my arm to start swimming, I felt the push of a giant weight against my body. *Sharks don't push. They devour.* With a thundering splash, a colossal dolphin jumped straight out of the water and back towards me. My muscles started to relax. Dell and I were not about to be a meal ticket.

"It's a dolphin!" I yelled. "A dolphin!" No matter, Wendell kept swimming towards the shore. "For Heaven's sake, Dell, it's a dolphin—like Flipper!" The kid stopped paddling and spun his head around.

"Holy Cow! They're huge! Like the ones at Sea World!"

The two dolphins circled around us jumping and splashing. The one who bumped me continued to nuzzle and nudge me. Slowly, I found myself stroking its soft slippery back. Next thing I knew, it nudged me again, almost as if it was coaxing me to ride it. Then, without warning, it dove underneath me and I had no choice but to grab its fin and hang on.

Like a rocket, the thing jumped into the air before arching forward into the water. I held on as long as I could before I was completely submerged again.

"My God, Dell, this isn't instinctual. Someone trained these things."

By now the kid had gotten used to the giant creatures who thought we were their playmates. They nuzzled and splashed him before turning away from both of us and swimming quickly down the channel to the beach on the other side of the island. I watched as they bounced through the water before I said anything to Wendell.

The image of people riding on dolphins wasn't new to me. I'd seen Ancient Minoan frescos of them in Boston's Museum of Fine Arts but never really thought it was possible. Then again, how was that any different from Sea World?

"We should have tried to ride them," Wendell said. "It would be like hanging on to a wild bull only the worst thing that could happen would be getting wet and we're wet already!"

"We? In case you weren't looking, I *was* riding one. Well, hanging on anyway. Oh well. They're gone, now. Besides, I'm too exhausted to do anything else. We need to get to shore and rest for a while."

I didn't want to say anything to Wendell but I was really unnerved by how well those dolphins were trained. Whoever had control of them might be more dangerous than the inhabitants who needed to make a sacrifice to their gods.

The sun was getting lower in the sky and the air started to turn colder. We rested for a few minutes on some large rocks that jutted out into the channel.

"The water's warmer than the air, Dell. I think we should make our way out of here before it gets dark. The channel will take us to the sea and another beach."

"Do you think those guys are going to track me down?"

"Probably not but I have a really bad feeling about this. We need to find some glass or even parts of a broken mirror tomorrow. And without a source for the vibrations, we'll wind up in some third world country without passports. The only thing we can really count on is the light from the sun."

I could see the look on Wendell's face and I knew he wasn't ready to go back. Reaching over, I grabbed him by the wrist.

"When we get what we need, don't you *dare* try any funny stuff. I mean it. There *is* no Atlantis and the best thing we can hope for is to get the heck out of here before something worse happens. Understand?"

"Uh—huh."

I had heard that tone of voice before. Coming from my brother. It meant one thing and one thing only—Wendell Tyler Banton wasn't about to listen.

Chapter Fifteen:

Wendell

I thought my arms were going to fall off! That girl was worse than Aunt Eleanor. At least she wasn't telling me to clean-up my mess or take off my shoes because the carpets were just steamed. The only thing she said when I slowed down was "Keep swimming."

The channel got wider and I swear it almost looked like a lake by the time it opened into the ocean. At least the current was going in our direction. I don't know if I crawled out onto the beach or if the current swept me in, spitting me on the sand. I was so freakin' tired that I fell right into the sand. Even got some in my mouth. Aeden said something like "you'll get over it," as she waited for me to stand up.

The sky was still light enough for us to start walking down the beach even though the sun had already set. I was freezing my butt off.

"I'm going to freeze to death, you know."

"And whose fault is that, Dell? If you haven't noticed, all I'm wearing is this lightweight dripping wet tunic from the costume department, so don't you dare complain to me."

"Take it easy, lady . . . uh . . . I mean Miss Aeden."

We rounded a curve on the beachfront and stopped dead in our tracks. Aeden grabbed my forearm and stood absolutely still.

"Shh. Take a look. It's a campfire, or at least the embers from one. Someone might be nearby. Stay still for a minute."

We waited long enough until we were sure it was safe. Aeden started walking slowly towards the spot as she spoke.

"No one's there. We can get that fire going again and keep warm. There's all sorts of driftwood on this beach. It's still light enough to do it."

"Barely," I mumbled, but she didn't hear me or pretended not to.

"Dell, take a look at this!"

She was pointing to a pile of rocks behind the campfire. At first I didn't see what the big deal was all about.

"Huh?"

"This is our lucky night! Whoever started this campfire left all sorts of stuff. See for yourself. There's vases stuck in the sand near the rocks and leftover fruits and fish. This must have been a 'party' spot earlier in the evening."

It didn't take us long to drink the watered down wine and eat a bunch of figs, grapes, and oranges. By the time we were done, only the dried fish remained.

The driftwood kept the fire going and our clothes dried before we fell asleep on the sand. It wasn't until the sunlight started to burn my eyelids that I woke up. Aeden had already put out the fire.

"Good. You're up and so is the sun. We can get going. The beach curves around a bend. Maybe we'll find some pieces of glass and get ourselves home. The waves vibrate. We can use that."

I was half-asleep but staggered along next to her as we approached the curve along the shore. I was looking down at the sand and noticing that it wasn't red like the other beach. Suddenly, Aeden let out a yell and I looked up.

"My God! Do you see that? It's unbelievable!"

In the distance was the biggest freakin' city I could imagine. Large whitewashed buildings everywhere and some sort of stadium in the middle of all of it. Parts of the city jutted out into the ocean and I could see more of those crescent shaped boats.

"You don't think . . . ?"

"No, I don't, Dell. It's got to be the ancient city of Thera. And the place we left, the one with the red beach, that has to be Akrotiri. It's the only explanation I can think of. Good. We'll keep going. We're bound to find what we need before we get too close to the city. We can't risk having anyone see us."

"I think it's too late for that."

"What do you mean?"

"Look over there!"

I pointed to some boulders a few yards from where we were standing. Someone had seen us and took off running back towards the channel. Aeden saw them, too.

"Change of plans, kid. We've got to get into that city and try to blend in. We can't risk getting dragged back to the other side of the island. And don't complain about how tired you are because I'm not in the mood to listen."

I didn't say anything but I did call her a name under my breath. One that would get me a week's worth of detentions.

Chapter Sixteen:

Aeden

Wendell Tyler Banton was insufferable. Spoiled, whiny and sneaky. He hadn't tried anything yet but that was only because we were running for our lives. I hated to think what that kid would do otherwise.

There was no time to stop and look for any shards of glass. We had to get into that city and hope that it was so crowded that no one would recognize us. The only trouble was my clothing. From what I remembered about studying Ancient Greece, and I figured the Minoans were close enough, slaves didn't wander about. If they were at a marketplace or on a street, it was to do someone's bidding and do it quickly. Wendell's attire was fine. Apparently the loincloth was as common as a pair of jeans. Lucky him.

The loose sand was everywhere, making it impossible to move quickly down the beach.

"Run closer to the water," I yelled. "The sand's

packed tighter."

Wendell grumbled but kept up with me.

"What do we do when we get there?"

Gee, Wendell, I'm not so sure. Let me take a look at our itinerary and see what the tour guide recommends.

What did he think we were going to do there? We'd have to make sure we weren't being followed before we could get to another beach and hopefully out of here. It was getting more complicated by the minute; and the fact that I was in slave garb didn't help. I bit my tongue and spoke.

"First thing *you're* going to do is to sneak around their marketplace and look for something that resembles a woman's robe. A long, narrow piece of rectangular material that will cover this tunic. Make sure it's a printed design and not a plain white one with a color on the hem. It can't be plain white with a color on the hem."

I could swear the kid's eyes were glazing over.

"Are you listening to me? It has to be a printed design."

"I get it. I get it. Printed design."

"That's right. Otherwise I might as well keep the one I'm wearing with the hem color announcing what household I belong to. I cannot be mistaken for a slave."

"OK, OK. Don't have a fit."

"Once you find something, grab it and start running to me wherever I'm hiding."

I couldn't believe I told this kid to do the very thing that got us into this mess in the first place. Only this time it wasn't information he would be stealing. He looked at me as if I just asked him to hijack a 747 and I had to admit, I never felt more conflicted in my life.

"Dell, this is not an ordinary circumstance. If someone mistakes me for a slave, we'll never get out of here. Understand? Just be quick about it."

Good going, Aeden. Maybe you can get him to play the Artful Dodger if the theater department decides to produce "Oliver."

A half dozen crescent shaped boats were visible off shore. We were getting closer to the city. Straight ahead I could see line after line of docks but it wasn't until we rounded a sharp curve that we saw exactly how enormous that city was. There had to be at least five channels cutting right through the place with buildings and vendors alongside. I'd never seen anything like it in my life.

Gargantuan statues of bulls, dolphins, and birds towered over the docks. Each of them held large oil lamps, enough to illuminate the entire bay. A giant glass orb, held in place by two bronze hands, made the oil lamps look small in comparison. It had to be a beacon for the boats. I wondered if it was visible only during the day when the sun hit it or if it emitted light in the darkness.

To our right, on a huge knoll, stood a three story arena with ornate columns and balconies. Behind it, houses and streets as far as the eye could see. The city of Thera was no longer buried under centuries of dirt. No longer a footnote in Wikipedia. We were staring right at it. I could see the look on Wendell's face as he took in the magnificence of the place.

"I know. I know." I said. "Pretty amazing for the Bronze Age, huh? Don't be getting any ideas about---."

For someone who spent the past hour complaining how his legs were cramping, Wendell suddenly had a burst of energy and took off before I could finish my sentence. I didn't bother yelling. He wouldn't have listened anyway. I shot off after him and used every bit of strength I had to knock him onto the sand.

"What the---?"

"You're lucky that's all I did. You don't go running off like that, you hear? Listen carefully. I'm going to stay back here behind this small hill. That city is bustling with people. Look how crowed the alleyways near the docks are! Find a vendor who's selling linen and grab a long colored robe. That's it! Don't fiddly-diddle around. Get it and get back here. It's so crowded that no one will notice you. Unless of course, you call attention to yourself, so don't."

"Yeah, yeah. I get it. I get it."

I watched as Wendell raced towards the city. It would be impossible for me to find him in that crowd and my stomach began to churn. What if he decided to do something really stupid? Worse than stealing. Then what? I tried not to think about it as I sank down into the soft sand on the side of the hill. Then, I had an even worse thought. What if these people needed a sacrificial victim, too? Would they take one look at Wendell and decide that he was going to be their gift to the gods? I bit my lip and stared at the crescent shaped boats.

You shouldn't have sent him off like that, Aeden. You should have known better.

Chapter Seventeen:

Wendell

"Don't fiddly-diddle!" She sounded like Aunt Eleanor. That's exactly what my aunt would have said. Well, cut me some slack, lady. I was almost offered up to the gods. I could have serious psychological issues after this!

It was like a madhouse the closer I got to the city. The smell of the sea and the beach all but disappeared. Instead, I could smell food roasting and some weird flowery perfume in the air. Aeden was right. There were so many vendors and so many people that I was elbow to elbow with them in the narrow walkways. No one saw me grab one of the sticks with roast chicken on it and stuff it in my mouth before taking off.

The juices slid down the corners of my mouth and I wiped them with my hand as I kept looking for that stupid robe she wanted. *"Make sure it's a printed design."* What the heck? I wasn't going into Target for crying out loud! When no one was looking, I grabbed a bunch of grapes from another stall and kept moving. Suddenly, everyone seemed to get out of the way and I was shoved back against a stall where the guy was selling some sort of icky cheeses. As I turned to see what was going on, at least twenty kids about my age ran past me shouting and waving red, gold and yellow banners in the air. Apparently the colors of the day on this island.

The cheese guy gave me a push and next thing I knew I was in the middle of the group. I couldn't turn around, I couldn't go back, I couldn't do anything except join them as they ran down the alley waving and shouting. I figured once they got out of the marketplace I could turn around and make a run for it. I was wrong. Dead wrong. Whatever this was, we were getting more and more boys to join us. I was wedged between two taller kids and had nowhere to go. So much for "don't fiddly-diddle around."

The moving flash mob never slowed down, running through narrow streets and across wide courtyards that were filled with people screaming and shouting. When we finally started to slow down I was inside the huge arena and it was pandemonium. Pushing, elbowing, shoving and cheering. Like a tailgate party gone wild. A shorter kid shook me by the wrist and pointed to a corral on my left. Boys about my height were going into it.

These people are insane. What the heck is going on? As I started to move towards that corral I got a better look at the place. There were at least four corrals, each one filling up with boys. It made *The Hunger Games* look mild. There was no escape from where I was standing and I didn't feel like getting trampled. I took my place in the corral and waited to see what was next.

I didn't have to wait long. Once all the boys were separated into the corrals, four bulls were brought into the arena. I always thought bulls were black, but in this case, they were red, white and brown with long horns and spitting mad faces. *A bullfight? A freaking bullfight? Is that what this is?* I tried to move to the back of the corral in case someone got the idea to throw me into the arena first but I couldn't elbow my way past the others.

I was right in front, alongside four or five other kids. Not bad odds but not the best either. Maybe these kids had some matador training but I sure as hell didn't. The closest I've ever been to a bull was in the back seat of a car as my father drove past a cow pasture in Connecticut.

Don't pick me. Don't pick me. I kept my eyes on the arena as I felt my entire body tremble. Seconds later, someone resembling Steven Seagal approached us. I could tell by what he was wearing that he was one of the guys in charge of this spectacle. *Don't pick me.* I held my breath as he got closer. Behind him, the bulls were kicking the sand and waiting. A piece of the roast chicken that I had snatched came back in my throat and for a brief second, I thought I was going to heave my guts out.

As I closed my eyes and swallowed, the man made his choice.

Chapter Eighteen:

Kitane, Courtyard of her home, 1750 B.C., Island of Thera

I tried to toss my bushy curls behind my ears as I raced through the small corridor that led to the courtyard. Mother would be furious that I didn't wait for my nurse to put the perfumed oil on my head and comb my hair so that each strand would hang gracefully from my head. I didn't even bother with my earrings. How could I?

Father's voice was bellowing from the courtyard. I had never heard him that angry before. Not even when a slave was careless and broke an expensive piece of pottery. Or even when a slave was caught stealing. This was different. All of our house slaves, with the exception of my nurse, and the one for my little brothers, had been summoned to the courtyard. My mind was racing. I had to find out what was happening.

I hid behind one of the large columns and

watched as Father paced in front of the slaves. Two of our centurions stood back near the center fountain. Judging from their faces, I knew that they had been admonished prior to this gathering. Holding my breath, I waited for Father to speak.

"A terrible darkness will befall this house and all the inhabitants of our island. We have angered the gods. Yesterday, the sea gifted us with a sacrifice for the gods. All preparations were made and the gift was taken to the holy spot that casts its eye on the volcanoes. The gods were ready to receive our offering at the noonday sun. Alas! Evil, taking on the form of a kitchen slave, set our gift free. Now, I fear we will no longer have rain in its season, and the volcanoes will rumble and spew their anger at us. No one will rest until our gift is returned and the demonic slave destroyed."

Father went on to explain that boats were already scouring the coast of our island for the dark haired boy and the slave girl. The girl would be easiest to recognize. She didn't have the long dark curls that were common on our island. Neither did she look like an Egyptian slave that might have been traded for goods. When Father described her, I knew immediately who she was.

On the morning when we buried Kitanetos, my grandfather, for whom I am named, I saw that slave sitting on the beach. She must have run ahead of our procession. Disobeying. Why didn't anyone see how evil she was? Poor Father, having to explain that the wrath of the gods would be upon us. I later learned that our bravest men were sent on the overland paths to the grand city of Thera where they would search indefinitely until they found our offering and the demon slave girl.

"Kitane, go back to your room immediately. You are not dressed appropriately to be about the courtyard!" My mother walked towards me pointing her finger at the corridor that led to my room.

"Do you think Father will find the gift offering and the demon before the grand Ceremony of the Bulls in Thera?" I asked.

"We must all pray to the gods that he does," Mother said as she walked with me towards my room. "You are of the age for a suitor, Kitane. You are fourteen years old. I was married by the time I was fifteen. It will be expected that your father selects your suitor from among the champions of the arena at the Taurokathapsia. The most able boys from the wealthiest families on the island will be competing. Our house has a fine reputation and no doubt you will be highly sought after. I trust your father will make the right choice for you."

"I don't want a suitor," I said as I brushed the unruly curls from my forehead. "I don't want to be married."

"Nonsense. It has already been decided. At the conclusion of the Taurokathapsia your betrothal will be announced. Now get to your room and finish dressing."

My brothers, Duripi and Nashuja, were lucky. They were still toddlers. When they grew older, they'd have choices. My fate was already sealed. Unless I could make sure that the gift from the sea and the demon girl who rescued him were never found. There would be no weddings and no celebrations if the gods were angry at us.

Chapter Nineteen:

Wendell

I didn't heave my guts out. Not at that moment anyway. The kid next to me was picked. I watched as he ran straight in front of the bull and jumped high enough to grab its horns before getting butted to the ground and nearly trampled to death under its hooves. He was escorted out of the arena as the next kid was thrown into the ring. I counted thirteen in all before it was my turn.

Only one guy made it to some sort of reserved area in front. He was the only one who didn't land on his butt or worse when he grabbed the bull. He had enough strength to hoist himself over the back of the bull and into the air before skidding off. Apparently, that's what this was all about. Or at least it seemed that way.

It looked as if the same thing was going on in the other corrals. The only difference was the size of the boys and the bulls. Sweat was pouring down my face as the number of boys in my corral dwindled. I knew I was next.

Ain't no big deal, Dell T. All you've got to do is jump, grab the horns and then run away as fast as you can. They'll throw you off this team.

By the time the gate latched behind me, the bull was in a really foul mood. He stomped the ground with one leg and glared at me like I was an insect that needed to be crushed. I moved my eyes from side to side looking frantically for a way out even though I knew I was trapped.

Just freakin' do it, Dell T. They don't expect you to succeed. Run over, jump, grab the horns and split. It can't be any worse than pull-ups.

All I could think of was a Band-Aid. I could pull it off slowly and feel every excruciating burn on my skin or I could yank it off in one second and be done with it. I went with the yank and raced towards that bull without stopping. What I didn't count on was that he raced towards me, too!

You moronic beast! You didn't pull this crap with the other kids. Why me?

I thought I jumped but I honestly don't know. What I do remember was grabbing the horns just as the bull bent his head forward and tossed my body into the air. I tucked my head down and somehow somersaulted over the back of the bull, sliding off his rump and onto the ground. It was worse than having the wind knocked out of me in a fight.

Great! I'm alive. I did it. Now get me the heck out of here.

Standing up, I began to wipe the sand off of my legs and walk out of the arena, no different than what the other loser kids did. Aeden would be pitching a fit but I could still get her stupid tunic and make it back to the beach.

No sooner did I take four or five steps when the Steven Seagal guard grabbed my arm, patted me on the shoulder and walked me to the special reserved area where five or six other boys were standing. Someone handed me a red, gold and blue sash that I was supposed to drape over my shoulder.

Did I win? What on earth did I win? I've got to get out of here!

By now the sun was full up in the sky and I could feel the heat on my head. Two-handled cups with watery wine were being passed around and the boys who were standing with me were cheering and congratulating each other.

Good. When does this end? When can I leave?

As it turned out, I didn't have to wait that much longer. Only one or two other kids made it to the special area. The others were sent away in shame and oddly enough, for the first time in my life, I wanted to be sent away in shame, too. It would have been the better option.

Next thing I knew, the gates to the arena were opened and this enormous screaming crowd ran in as if Miley Cyrus was giving a free concert. It was insane. Totally out of control. For some reason, I pictured Aunt Eleanor complaining about the crowds in the mall on Black Friday. *"Honestly, Wendell, I thought my nails would chip."*

People stormed towards us clanging cymbals and tossing grapes into the air. It was the kind of free-for-all I pictured after the Super Bowl only without the beer. Suddenly, I felt two arms lifting me by the waist. In an instant, I was above the crowd, on someone's shoulders and we were heading out of the arena. As I looked around me, the other kids with the colored sashes were on people's shoulders, too. Whatever the heck I won, it must have been epic.

We were carried down the narrow streets with humongous crowds of people on either side. The girls were throwing flowers and leaves but a few pomegranates were hurled our way as well. It was impossible to hear anything over all the screaming and yelling.

Dell T, you're in a victory parade! Deal with it!

The parade, or whatever you want to call it, had to end soon. It was getting ridiculous. I held on to whoever was carrying me through the city and looked straight ahead. We were approaching the plaza by the docks and I couldn't believe what I was seeing. Bonfires with different colored flames were everywhere. I had the uneasy feeling that this was only the start of the celebration. I'd never be able to get Aeden's tunic and make it back to the beach before dark. It was a sea of people. Bobbing and wadding in front of me. All of the faces were beginning to look alike. All except the one I saw a few feet from me.

My stomach tightened and I felt woozy. I was about to barf and there was nothing I could do to stop it.

Chapter Twenty:

Aeden

The sun was almost overhead and there was no sign of Wendell. He was probably having the time of his life wandering around that marketplace helping himself to all sorts of food and treats and who-knows-what-else. I could kick myself for even thinking he could handle something as simple as snatching a robe and making a run for it. Exotic fruits, spices, sweets . . . He'd be the proverbial kid in a candy shop. Worse than my mother at IKEA. What possessed me to send him off alone? It was a stupid move.

I had already thrown sand on the fire to extinguish it and managed to wash up in the warm surf. This side of the island seemed so much warmer than the one with the red beach. Not a good thing since the hot sun was already making me uncomfortable. There was no real shade either. Only a few small olive trees and some bushes here and there amid the rocks. The only high point was when I found an earring on the beach. I knew that women who were not slaves wore them and if I could get my hair to curl a bit, maybe no one would notice that I was missing the other one.

Of course I needed to be wearing something other than slave garb, and given the fact that Wendell hadn't returned yet, I was stuck. Not only that, but I was getting worried. What if something really bad did happen to him? I scanned the beach and looked for any sign of movement. Nothing.

Congratulations Aeden. You win the award for being totally irresponsible. Sending a fourteen year-old kid into a Bronze Age marketplace? Especially that kid!

Biting my lip as I wiped the beads of sweat from my eyes, I started walking in the direction of the city. I had to find Wendell, steal a robe and get us back to our own time. Wendell had it easy. He left before the sun was fully up. I was walking with it dead overhead. To make matters worse, the sand was getting hot and I had to stay close to shore where the pieces of broken shells and fish bones kept getting into my sandals.

My mind would alternate between anger at Wendell and fear for his life. That dialogue played out like a bad daytime TV drama.

"He could be lying on another slab waiting to be sacrificed!"

"Or he could be stuffing his face with grapes and dates."

"What if the guards from the other side of the island found him?"

"Could he be idiotic enough to be looking for clues to Atlantis?"

"Chances are he's bound and gagged by now. Waiting to be offered to the gods."

By the time I got close enough to the outskirts of the city, I was a total wreck. I promised myself that I wouldn't read him the riot act if I found him alive and well, but it turned out to be one promise that I broke without reservation.

Large whitewashed villas began to dot the landscape. I selected the one that had a small retaining wall so that I could easily duck behind it if I needed to do so. From there, I could go villa to villa until I reached the center of the city. It seemed really strange that there was no one in sight. Not in the yard, not near the small decorative ponds, and not in the courtyards. I walked quietly and cautiously, darting my eyes in both directions.

If it wasn't for the chatter of a few birds in the small trees, the silence would have been unnerving. I followed the wall, skirting around the villa as I glanced into its atriums and courtyards. At first I thought I was merely looking at some bright tiles near one of the fountains but when

I got closer, I became ecstatic. It was clothing! One of their slaves left clothes out to dry in the sun!

OK, so maybe it wasn't exactly like a great sale at Marshalls or T.J. Maxx, but it was bargain day for me. I hoisted myself over the wall and took a look. Sure enough, there were colorful vests and flowing skirts in reds, yellows, and blues. White sashes with symmetrical designs were also drying in the heat. Wasting no time, I stepped into a skirt and put one of the vests on. They were meant to be open and I hoped that the sash I grabbed would cover my bare skin. Unlike the Romans, the Minoan women who were not slaves were free to expose their navels. They'd fit right in at Venice Beach. So much for trying to find a tunic. At breakneck speed, I slipped out of the slave costume and balled it up. When I climbed back over the wall, I found a thick clump of bush and stashed the costume underneath it, making sure that it wasn't visible.

You can relax now, Aeden. No one will think you're a slave. Of course, things might be a tad different for Wendell . . .

I couldn't get my mind to stop churning up the worst images. Quickly, I raced past that villa and through two more until I realized why they weren't filled with people. It was the rumble of noise near the city that got my attention and gave me the answer. Everyone had poured into the city streets, plazas and docks. Music, laughter, screaming and shrieking replaced the solitary chirp of the birds. It was followed by the most intense aromas I could imagine. Even more so than the ones that permeated the air in that fishing village.

Unafraid of being caught this time, I headed straight for the city center. There was no doubt in my mind that I'd find Wendell in the middle of all the excitement. What I didn't expect was that he would be such an integral part of it.

Chapter Twenty-one:

Kitane

When my tutor wasn't looking, I snuck behind our villa to the spot where the old musician had been banished until the next moon. He was too frail for a beating according to Father but had been exiled from the rest of the villa because he let the demon girl steal our gift offering to the gods.

I had to learn more about this girl so that I could find her before father's men did. If she was returned to us, I feared she would have no recourse but to bring our sacrificial gift back. The gods would be pleased and my betrothal would be announced. Father would select the finest champion from the Taurokathapsia and I would be forced to spend the rest of my life as a married woman. I spit on the ground three times to banish that thought from my mind.

Father was adamant that the gods would destroy our island if they didn't receive that sacrifice; and I certainly didn't want destruction to reign down upon us either. The only difference was that I didn't think the gods would stay angry forever. No one does. In time, they would bring back the rain for the crops and let our volcanoes sleep peacefully.

My only chance at happiness meant that the gods would be hostile. I decided to take that chance and find out where the demon girl had gone. The elderly slave didn't notice me at first so I paused to listen to his melancholy music. Each note hung in the air like an omen. Clearing my throat, I spoke.

"I am Kitane, daughter of the household, and I have come for information."

"I know who you are and you should not be here. There is little I can tell you that I have not shared with your father."

"Do you know where the demon girl has gone? What path she took?"

"The one that took her back to the underworld. I have never seen a look as fierce as the one on that girl's face. Sharp. Determined. She would walk on the bodies of the dead to suit her aims."

"So she did not take one of the paths to the city?"

"It would have been impossible. She would have been caught. The demon girl leapt over the volcanoes and into the underworld. I looked behind me as I ran down the hill and she disappeared into the clouds."

I glanced toward the hills and the three volcanoes.

"I hope you will return in good time to our villa. Surely your music will be missed."

It was my way of thanking him even though I didn't believe that the girl went into the underworld. That was a place where only snakes sent by the Mother Goddess dwelled. No, the demon girl had found a way over the volcanoes and I wondered if it was possible for me to do the same.

The walkway leading up to the sacred ritual stone was not too far from where I was already standing. I knew that my tutor would be too scared to tell my mother that he had failed to keep a close eye on me. That meant no one would be looking for me. Not right away. It was still early afternoon. I looked back at the house and gardens before making my way on the rutted, rocky path.

I had never been to this spot. The gods received their gifts from the heads of the households with the sacrifice made by the holiest of priests. When my brothers got old enough, our father would take them to witness such a ceremony.

The path narrowed and got steeper with each step that I took. At times I feared I would lose my footing and tumble beyond the edge of the hill. Still, it was a risk I had to take. Perhaps the girl had left a clue as to where she had gone and what she intended to do with our gift from the sea.

My feet moved steadily as I listened to the soft rustling of the breeze. Not too much further. I could see the rock staircase straight ahead. It didn't look like the one Father had described when I was a child. It looked narrower and more intimidating as it spiraled around the hill. I knew the sacred slab would be in the clearing once I reached the top.

The scent of the oil lamps that dotted the walkway still lingered in the air. I took a deep breath and began to climb the steps, lifting my legs higher and higher to accommodate for the increased height of each step. When I had finally reached the top of the spiral, I could see the holy place.

Two enormous oil lamps stood at the far end of the rock slab but I couldn't make out what the object was that rested between the slabs. Some sort of ceremonial bowl? I moved closer before stopping suddenly in my tracks.

It was a viper that immediately sprang to life from its coiled sleep, leaning its head forward and baring its fangs at my face. I jumped back before it had a chance to spring at me. In that instant I knew Father was right. We had angered the gods and now the Mother Goddess sent her centurion to keep watch over this holy place until the sacrifice could be made.

Chapter Twenty-two:

Aeden

I'd never seen a festivity like this. Not quite a parade, more like the aftermath from a big game or maybe even a concert. The crowd kept pushing its way to see something and I was swept along with it. I laughed at myself for worrying about the placement of a single earring and having to arrange my hair accordingly. No one was looking at me. Whatever they were straining to see took over everyone's senses. The cheering was deafening. Too bad I couldn't understand a word. Even so, it was definitely celebratory in nature. Not a funeral. Not a sacrifice.

A few yards from me I could make out ten or so boys being carried on the shoulders of larger men. Flowers and fruit were tossed in the air as they made their way down the street. I imagined Wendell was somewhere in the crowd watching as he helped himself to whatever he could snatch from the open air vendors. It was nearly impossible to scan for that little brat while being thrust closer and closer to the action.

Times Square on New Year's Eve couldn't compete with this. It was pure pandemonium. At least until the second when someone shoved me forward and I found myself staring straight at a sight that made my blood turn cold. It was Wendell. Wendell Tyler Banton on the shoulders of some tanned hulk who paraded the kid around as if he was showing off the greatest prize since the discovery of dirt.

My mouth dropped open and I stood there gaping at him. He had a bright blue, red and yellow sash across his chest and looked as if he was about to get an Olympic medal. He also looked as if he was going to throw-up. I rushed towards him and mouthed the words, *"What the heck?"* before knocking into the guy who had hoisted him up. In that split second, Wendell slid to the ground and began retching but the crowd was moving so fast that we were literally swept away from the aftermath of his upset stomach.

No one could hear us above the shouting and cheering. I was furious.

"All you had to do was grab a robe and get back to the beach. What's the matter with you?"

"I was nearly gored to death by a bull!"

"WHAT?"

"Yeah, and I don't know what the hell is happening either!"

"You must have some idea. You're sitting on some guy's shoulders like you just won the Kentucky Derby!"

"Yeah, that. I think I sort of won a contest or something."

"What do you mean?"

Wendell started to explain about the corrals and the bull jumping but before he could finish, another huge man lifted him into the air as the crowd continued to cheer. The kid was back on someone's shoulders headed for who-knows-where and I had no choice but to follow him.

The celebration moved to the center plaza and the docks where I had seen the giant orb and the bronze lanterns. I could feel my stomach rumbling as I tried to keep up with the crowd, all the while not taking my eyes off of Wendell. Off to the side I could see trays of meats and delicacies being carried towards the public square. I was ravenous.

The afternoon sun was slowly setting and the docks took on an eerie glow as lantern lights illuminated the area. A large circle of tables quickly filled with these bull jumping champions who were now being served the wine and roasted meats. Wendell caught the look on my face and shrugged as he popped something into his mouth.

I had all I could do to keep myself from choking the daylights out of him.

As it turned out, the champions weren't the only ones who were offered food. They were just the only ones who were seated. Within minutes, slaves from all over the city wove in and out of the crowd with platters of fish, fruit, and meats. I helped myself to anything that was within reaching distance, including dried octopus in some sort of sauce.

Tomatoes and grapes quenched my thirst as I watched the spectacle in front of me. It was nearly dark by the time the crowd started to dissipate. I figured Wendell and I could slip away to the beach for another night before getting back to our own time. I was wrong.

The boys were led back through the city in two lines that wove through the streets until culminating in front of a large villa. I moved as quickly as I could to get within ear reach of Wendell.

"What's going on? People were talking to you while you were eating. You understand the language. What did they say?"

"I was selected to compete in some sort of rodeo or marathon," he whispered. "Something with bulls and fighting. I'm not *that* good with their language."

"When? When do you compete?"

"In six or seven days. I'm not so good with their numbers either."

"And in the meantime?"

"All of us stay here and practice whatever it is we have to do."

"My God, Dell. I don't know if---"

Just then, one of the guards who accompanied the boys motioned for me to leave. I didn't wait to be told a second time. I stepped back but not before mouthing the words, "Try to escape!"

Chapter Twenty-three:

Kitane

No one noticed that I had been gone most of the afternoon. Mother was too busy selecting her wardrobe for the Taurokathapsia and ordering her slaves to arrange everything neatly on the linen rolls so that her things could be easily moved onto the boat for our excursion to Thera. It was only a matter of time before she would get to me and begin that process with my slaves. My stomach was in knots.

My brothers didn't realize how lucky they were to remain home while my parents and I went to the other side of the island for this event. Mother felt that they were too young to witness the spectacle in the arena. The same couldn't be said for me. I had been to the Ceremony of the Bulls three times before but never under such a cloud as the one that was now hanging over my head.

I didn't care which champion Father selected.

I wanted no part of it. Betrothal would mean the end of everything I loved. No more swimming with the dolphins or walking down the beach at dawn. I'd have to live in my husband's household until such time as I had children and ran my own villa. Most likely Father would select someone from a merchant fisherman family like ours where they had small boats for island fishing and larger vessels that sailed to the distant lands for trade.

I thought about how awful it would be if I was forced to wash my husband's feet like wives do in those lands beyond the islands. Sitting on a cushion near the balcony of my room, I stared at the turquoise sky, jumping to attention the moment I heard my mother's footsteps on the tile.

"You and I will be dining in the atrium tonight, Kitane. Your father has business to attend to and your brothers have already been fed."

"Is it about the ceremony in Thera?"

"Yes, the arrangements are being made now. The boat will leave at dawn the day after tomorrow. You may take only one of your slaves so I suggest you pick the girl who can best style your hair. We will be staying with one of the royal families at their villa just outside the city."

I didn't say anything. I just turned back to face the balcony. My mother continued to speak in low, serious tones.

"In time you will come to understand that your Father has made the right choice. You will have one year of betrothal. The wedding to take place the month preceding the next festival of the bulls."

"Mother, I---"

"Not a word, Kitane. Call your slaves and direct them to prepare your wardrobe. You are to dress in your finest skirts and vests with the appropriate adornments. Make sure that the girls fold your clothing neatly into the linen wraps."

I nodded as she continued.

"Once we arrive in Thera, our hosts will expect us to attend the banquet they have prepared. You are to display proper manners and stay within the villa at all times. Young girls of age may never go out alone in the streets without being accompanied by a family member or one of their slaves. Do you understand?"

"I do, but---"

"Then I have made myself clear. I will expect you in the atrium at dusk. It would be wise if you were to begin selecting your wardrobe. Good afternoon, Kitane."

I stood up and walked towards the small anteroom where my clothing was kept. I liked to wear my bodices and tunics loose fitting over my skirts so that I could run freely about. That certainly would not meet Mother's approval. She would want them tight to show-off the curves around my chest and waist. And I wouldn't be able to wear the shorter skirts either. She'd insist on the long bell shaped ones that made me feel as if I was being stuffed into a vase. I chose the long, colorful ruffled shirts with crimson, blue and gold bands and hoped she wouldn't be too angry.

If I remembered correctly, the Taurokathapsia lasted three days. Well, three days for the public event. I think Father once told me that the preparation for the competition ran another two or three days. The boys were selected from a preliminary trial and then underwent special training to prepare them for the arena. No one was allowed to watch that part of the festival. I know I certainly didn't want to watch a bunch of smelly, oily boys run around with bulls, especially if one of them turned out to be my husband. Still, I had time. The demon girl hadn't been found yet. I would have heard the news from the slave chatter the minute I returned from the sacred spot.

Yes, I had time. Even if it was only two days. I would scour the streets of Thera and all its beaches to find her. As I left the anteroom, I smiled. I knew which slave girl I was taking and it wasn't the one who could style my curls. It was the one whose legs were built like rams and who could race up the volcano path without losing her breath. She would need to do so in order to keep up with me.

Chapter Twenty-four:

Wendell

"Try to escape?" Was she nuts? The place was surrounded by guards. I didn't even think a Navy Seal team could break in. We were outnumbered. At least two guards for each one of us "bull rodeo champs." I did a quick head count and came up with nineteen of us lucky winners. There may have been a few more, or a few less, but I was close enough. We ranged in height by a few inches and it looked as if most of us were between 13–18 years old.

I looked around the large courtyard with its even bigger fountain in the shape of a dolphin's mouth and realized something—I seemed to fit in with my longish hair. These guys weren't bald like the ones on that boat. One thing for sure, the party was over. We were immediately directed to small rooms that surrounded the fountain. Good thing there was enough light from the oil lamps on the walls and the lanterns in the courtyard or

I would have been stumbling around the place.

A few of the guards seemed to be yelling at once and next thing I knew, a passel of slaves showed up to escort us to our rooms in case we couldn't figure it out for ourselves. I got to share my room with two other kids. Three cots, one against each wall, were covered with linens and cushions. A small rectangular table with some fruits and vases of what I figured must be wine was in the middle of the room. So much for amenities.

I took the cot that was directly under the window just in case there was the slightest chance I could climb out. (There wasn't). As I turned my head to gauge the distance between the bed and the window, one of the slaves began to take off my sandals and wash my feet. I nearly jumped out of my skin. The other guys were getting their feet washed, too. Then, one by one they introduced themselves—Yidini and Sima. Without thinking, I started to say my full name but got as far as "Wen" and Yidini finished it for me—Widina. Apparently I lucked out and Widina was a real name.

Yidini, as it turned out, was a talker. He babbled and babbled about stuff. Sima would add a few words here and there and I would mostly nod and say "vai" for yes. Both of them came from other parts of the island. Or maybe other islands. I wasn't so sure. What I was sure of was the fact that we were going to be trained for some big deal competition involving the bulls.

Words like "running," and "jumping" were used over and over again. I had the feeling that this was going to be like a bullfight, only worse. I didn't think matadors had to jump over their bulls so maybe I was missing something. I glanced back at the window, wishing it was two or three feet lower. I just hoped that whatever red cape they gave me would be big enough for me to duck under.

The thought of being gored by a bull made me lose what little appetite I had left. Yidini and Sima, on the other hand, acted like they had just made it to the NCAA. I pretended to yawn and lean back on my cot when one of the guards returned, said something and proceeded to blow out the oil lamps in our room. Other than the fact that this might have turned out to be my last night on earth, it was Camp Mohegan all over again.

"Lights Out Campers! Lights Out!"

Terrific. Nothing like lying in the dark contemplating the activities someone lined up for you the next day. Swimming? Boating? Tennis? Hiking? I let out a slow breath as I went down the list: running for your life, getting gored, getting trampled, and getting killed. Maybe Yidini and Sima were looking forward to a good night's sleep but all I could think about was how I was going to survive the next day. Camp Mohegan was a paradise compared to this.

Lights out for you, Dell T!

Chapter Twenty-five:

Aeden

I stepped back into the crowd seconds before the guards closed the gates to the villa. Wendell turned quickly and shrugged, then raced to catch up to the other boys. By now the sun had set and the only light emanating from the courtyard of the villa was the glow from the oil lamps. Outside, on the streets, there was enough lantern light for the festival-goers as they made their way home. Some of them held torches, making it easier for the rest of us to see where we were going. Not that it mattered to me. I had no idea where I was going. The thought of spending another night on the beach sent a chill down my spine. It was a long walk and I doubted I could maneuver it in the dark.

Thankfully, I didn't have to. No sooner did I turn away from the villa when a girl looped her arm around my elbow, moving quickly towards three or four other girls who were laughing and giggling. Somehow she thought I belonged with them and I wasn't about to give her any reason to doubt that.

The girls all looked to be in their mid to late teens and all of them were wearing clothing similar to mine—long ruffled or bell shaped skirts with bodices that opened in front. The only difference was that they had lots of necklaces to cover their bare chests. I had to make do with a sash that I pressed against me for fear of having it slip to the ground. Heck, I didn't even like wearing bikinis. Worse yet, this outfit made 21st-century swimwear look like it came out of the Victorian Age.

No matter. I was in style and not mistaken for a slave. With our elbows linked together like partners in a square dance, we cut through the crowd and wove our way through the winding streets. The girls were singing, laughing and dancing until at last we were standing in front of an absolutely enormous villa that looked more like a palace. One of the girls said something to the guards who were standing in front and they immediately opened the gates for us.

Within seconds, two slave girls appeared, handed us gold ribbons for our wrists and motioned for us to follow them. For a brief second it reminded me of having to wear a wrist band for a Taylor Swift concert. Was that what this was? Some sort of admission ticket? I tied it on my right wrist and followed them inside.

In the dim lamp light I could see that the courtyard walls were painted in symmetrical designs. The bold colors even managed to stand out in the shadows. We walked past gardens and archways until we got to a narrow corridor with smaller archways. A few more slave girls appeared and showed us to a large room with small tables of food and drink. *Good going, Aeden. You hit pay dirt. Just don't blow it.*

It didn't take me long to figure out that I was apparently someone's guest. We were all guests of whoever owned this palatial estate. Whatever this event was that Wendell got himself into, it was of such magnitude and importance that guests were being housed in the finest Minoan villas and estates. I just wished I understood what the heck my new girlfriends were saying.

This was a hundred times worse than Paris. At least I knew some French words like *yes* and *no,* as well as certain items off of a menu. Well, no *omelette au fromage* for me. Their language sounded like a jumble of vowels mixed with guttural sounds. The only thing I could do was smile, try to listen carefully, and repeat a few words here and there.

Luckily, the girls all seemed to be talking at once so no one noticed that I wasn't contributing to the conversation. I stood up to help myself to some grapes when one of the girls pointed to my missing earring. *You've played Charades before, Aeden. Don't just stand there like a ninny.*

I immediately touched my hand to the lobe where the earring should have been and acted surprised and upset. The girl said something and then reached for a small pouch that she had tucked into her bodice. Opening it carefully, she showed me all sorts of gold earrings with stones and pearls. Then, she took one out that sort of resembled the one in my other ear and handed it to me.

Not knowing if I should give her a hug, shake her hand or bow my head, I grasped her hand in mine for just a second and gave it a quick squeeze before slipping the earring through the bottom of my lobe. The girl stepped back and smiled just as one of the slaves cleared her throat and spoke.

Next thing I knew, we were following that slave down the corridor to a series of small guest rooms that were reserved for us. Two girls to each room. Stone slabs with layers of colorful cushions stood at opposite ends of the room. Sconces on the wall gave off enough light so that I could see the incredible murals on the wall. This time it wasn't the sea creatures and bulls I had come to expect. Instead, I was staring at the images of active volcanoes surrounded by plants and flowers.

The slave girl pointed out a large vase for washing and an archway with a linen drape over it. She pushed the drape aside to reveal what I assumed was the commode. Another archway led to our own outdoor courtyard. I took a step forward and gasped. In the distance I could see the outline of the city and the giant orb that stood over the docks. The villa where Wendell had been taken was a few yards from there. Surrounding it were the flames from torches that people were still carrying. It meant that they were still celebrating even though it was so late. I imagined Wendell had stuffed himself with more food and was sleeping comfortably. Then, the worst thought crept into my head and I shuddered. Was Wendell going to escape?

Second bad move you've made since you got here, Aeden. First, you send the kid off by himself to the big city and now you tell him to escape from a villa guarded by centurions on steroids. Don't count on a good night's sleep.

Chapter Twenty-six:

Wendell

At least I didn't pee the bed. The worst nightmares imaginable crept into my subconscious and messed with me all night long. Most of them involved me getting gored in the stomach by a bull the size of Lower Manhattan. In one of them some girl was dragging me to an altar and I couldn't be sure if I was going to be sacrificed or married. Compared to that dream, the bull goring was a pleasant pastime.

All of us woke up to the sound of one of the guards knocking on the wall by our archway. The sun wasn't even up yet. A slave who looked like he hadn't slept either came rushing in with towels and vases of water. Yidini held out his hands for the guy to wash and then proceeded to point out the other body parts in need of cleansing.

I immediately snatched one of the towels, poured water on it and started washing myself. Sima gave me a weird look and then sat down to wait for his turn to get a sponge bath from the slave.

While we were sleeping, someone had entered our room and placed clean loincloths on the small table near the door. I got into mine as quickly as I could while Yidini and Sima were getting towel dried. The two of them weren't even dressed yet when a different slave entered the room with a platter of cheese, some sort of bread, and fruits. I helped myself to an orange and the rounded flat bread.

Yidini and Sima had to choke down their food in a hurry because seconds later one of the centurions entered our room and directed us to head down the corridor to the courtyard. It was just sunrise when we found ourselves lined up in rows of three, facing the Steven Seagal guy from the arena. He was barking orders all over the place. Yep, I was back at Camp Mohegan. *You sissy boys from the city are going to shape up. We have calisthenics followed by dodge ball and foot races. Then you'll get in a quick swim before lunch. And don't let me catch any of you sneaking off to the latrine to read comic books!*

He spoke so loud and so fast that I only understood a few words, but those were enough. *Run, jump, horns, and either twist or tumble.* Either way, it wasn't looking too good. We were led out of the courtyard and marched across the city streets until we reached the huge arena. This time there was no parade. A few passersby looked up at us and then continued walking. I almost expected to see Aeden glaring at me and screaming, "I told you to escape." Not only that, but I had the strangest feeling that she was watching me. *Yeah, well, you try to escape from Thor and his pals!*

Unlike camp, there was no talking allowed as we moved along the streets. That was probably a good thing, since I didn't think I could actually carry on a decent conversation. When we got to the arena, it looked even bigger and more menacing than it did yesterday. The building seemed to stretch forever with three different seating levels, each of them framed by giant columns. One of the guards said something and our rows fanned out until we formed a long semi-circle on the edge of the ring. Then, a few tall muscular men stood in front of us and demonstrated exactly what we were supposed to do. So much for waving a cape. Maybe that came later. What we were shown was more like gymnastics. Gymnastics on a hard dirt floor. *Hey, you guys have cushions. Couldn't you at least have invented mats?*

The first guy held his arms straight up in the air and then leaned back until the top of his body was almost parallel with the ground. Ten seconds later he leaned forward, lifted one of his legs behind him, and did this weird handstand-cartwheel. If that wasn't enough, he did another one, this time from a dead run across the arena.

I knew we weren't all standing around to be entertained. *Training video one, Dell. Get it right.* A tanned guard, whose muscles bulged in all directions, walked directly in front of us and pointed to the first kid at the end of our semi-circle. Without saying anything, the kid tried to copy that maneuver. It took him three tries but once he got it, he was told to get back in line and sit on the ground.

Eight more kids tried. Amazingly, they were able to do it. *You could do this, too, Dell. You had to take those idiotic Presidential Fitness Tests. Hell, it's just a handstand with a tumble. At least they're not making you climb a rope. (No, that'll come later along with some sort of trapeze stunt!)*

I seriously thought about falling on my face but I wasn't too sure what they'd do to me. So, I took a deep breath, pretended I was back in elementary school, and managed to get it right on the second try. As I sat down on the hard dirt, I looked around the arena. Still no sign of a bull. Maybe that was a good thing.

It was mid-morning when they gave us a break. An entourage of slaves arrived with vases of wine, platters of dried fish and hard bread. We were also taken to a spot behind the arena where deep pits in the ground with the most awful stench were pointed out to us. I swore as long as I lived, I'd never complain about using a gas station toilet.

The rest of the afternoon was pretty much like the morning. Weird gymnastic moves that we had to learn quickly. We were all standing in that semi-circle sweating like pigs in a desert when it was finally over for the day. The guard who had directed the entire workout approached us. He was accompanied by a slave carrying a small basket of cloths. As the guard got to each one of us, he said something and the slave handed us one of the cloths. Mine was red. The other color was blue.

As I took my cloth and tied it to my loincloth like the kids before me did, the guard said two words. *Blood dance.* I wanted to beat myself over the head for ever learning Ancient Greek. Sometimes you're better off not knowing what's coming.

Chapter Twenty-seven:

Kitane

I slipped off my sandals so that my footsteps wouldn't make any noise on the cold tiles as I crossed the atrium into the large kitchen. Above me, only a few stars emitted any light. The clouds had obscured everything. The oil lamps were sufficient to cast an outline of the room. I was lucky last night. No one caught me. I wasn't so sure about this evening. Something didn't feel right.

I walked past the bread ovens and the wash stations until I reached the pantry area. It had taken me a long time yesterday to lift each of the small jars to find what I needed. I could only take a little bit so as not to arouse suspicion. Tonight I intended to add more. I would need it to bribe Father's men so that they wouldn't be so anxious to find that demon girl. *And what if they do find her, Kitane. Then what? Then I make sure she doesn't linger in Thera.*

The shelf was slightly above eye level and I had to be careful that my hand didn't slip and knock over something. Slowly, I took out the small jar that I held tightly in my hand, making sure not to tip it over as I removed the clay lid. Then, I began to pour some of the powdery substance from the kitchen spices into my own vessel.

I made sure the lid was on and started to return the jar to its place on the shelf. We would be leaving for Thera in the morning so I doubted anyone would miss the coveted saffron spice. I turned to step out of the pantry when the echo of footsteps crossing the atrium sent a quick chill down my back. There was no place to hide.

In the semi-darkness I watched as the night guard made his way into the kitchen.

"Kitane! What are you doing here? It is well past the midnight hour."

"I woke up hungry and wanted to eat some fruits. I knew where they kept the dried figs and helped myself to a handful."

"Your slave should have been sent to fetch you something."

"I know, but she was sleeping soundly and I didn't want to wake her."

If he thought I was lying, he gave no indication of it.

"Your mother would not be pleased if she

found out that you were roaming the corridors by yourself at night."

"Please do not say anything. She is angry enough at me. I don't want to go to Thera."

"I shall keep silent this time, Kitane. In the future, send your slave to the kitchen should hunger pangs awaken you. Come, I will escort you back to your room."

"That's not necessary. I can find my way."

"I would not be doing my duty if I were to let you return by yourself."

I thanked him and gripped the small jar tighter, holding it to my side, as he walked me back to the archway of my room. Once inside, I placed the jar amid my perfume vessels. In the morning I would find a way to tie it to my clothing. It was the one item the slaves were not going to pack for me.

Mother clapped her hands at the archway and I awoke with a start. The sun wasn't even up yet and my slaves hadn't arrived to see to my morning routine. Mother lit into me with a barrage of questions and demands before I finished yawning.

"Kitane! We will be leaving within the hour. Where is the slave girl who will be accompanying you? I trust all of your clothes are arranged. Two of our house slaves will be loading them onto our boat. Did you select the girl who knows how to apply makeup? I don't want you looking like a fishwife. Are you listening to me, Kitane?"

"I hear you, Mother."

"Good. Have your slaves fetch you something to eat and hurry up. Our litter is being prepared as we speak."

"I don't want to be carried through the streets like a spectacle."

"Well, you're most certainly not going to run down to the harbor as if you were a common slave. You need to know your place, Kitane. If you cannot make a good impression in our own city, I tremble at the thought of the one you will make in Thera."

"Will I be staying at the same quarters as you and Father once we get there?'

"You will be in the same palatial villa but not in our quarters. You are no longer a little girl. You are of age, Kitane. You shall be staying with the other young ladies in separate quarters."

I wanted to hold my tongue but I couldn't. The words came out before I could stop them.

"Are they also condemned to a betrothal or is it only Father who seeks a champion for me?"

My mother moved as if she were about to slap my face but suddenly stepped back and spoke.

"Your Father has two choices. He can sell

you as a slave or give you away as a bride. Be careful of the direction in which you push him."

An hour later I was gazing at the deep teal waters as our boat headed to Thera. The small jar of spice dangled innocently from my waist. Mother was pleased that I had decided to carry perfume with me, and I thanked the gods that she didn't wish to inhale its aroma.

Chapter Twenty-eight:

Aeden

I tossed and turned all night, getting up at intervals to look across the courtyard, half expecting to see Wendell stumbling around the streets. *He wouldn't be stupid enough to really try to escape in the middle of the night, would he?* I tried to convince myself that his daredevil antics only pertained to computer systems and there weren't any in 1750 B.C. Still, I couldn't sleep.

Finally, I gave up and decided to walk down the corridor of our villa in order to stretch my legs. I was thankful that I didn't have to share my room with anyone. It would have been impossible to explain what I was doing.

Dim oil lamps gave off an eerie yellow glow that lit up the frescos on the walls of the main courtyard. Alone in the semi-darkness, I studied the paintings as if they held some key to what was going on in this villa and the arena.

Each scene, with the exception of the one in which playful dolphins lifted riders into the air, was more disturbing than the next. Like the walls in my room, the landscapes all showed volcanoes erupting and covering the trees and plants with a firestorm of molten lava. Had there been such an eruption in their history or was this a prediction? Other scenes centered on bulls with acrobats tumbling around and over them. Some of the men appeared to be gored in the process while others narrowly escaped. Then, there were the fight scenes. Men brutally pummeling each other with their bare fists until one of them lay dead on the ground.

Finally, I eyed a bucolic scene with flowers and a woman dressed in her finery approaching a tall man in a bloody loincloth. Behind her, women were in a circle, dancing. All I could think of was the expression, "to the victor belong the spoils." Then, I realized what I was looking at and I froze. Wendell wasn't going to participate in a rodeo. He was about to be gored to death in some bizarre ritual celebration. I had to get to that villa and warn him.

Without wasting a second, I tip-toed back to my room and threw the long skirt and bodice over the lightweight tunic that I had worn to bed. It was one of the surprising amenities that the slave girls had brought us. I made my way past the great courtyard into the open corridor when I realized that guards would be stationed at the main door. The only alternative was to climb down the wall from my courtyard and make my way in the dark over the rocky ledge and dense brush.

I cursed Professor Heidecker. I cursed Wendell. And most of all, I cursed myself for being so brainless as to put those time travel formulas on my iPad. My arms got scraped as well as my ankles as I slithered down the courtyard wall past the brush and plants until I found myself on one of the streets that led to the docks where Wendell's villa was located.

It was barely past dawn when I saw his building a few yards from me. Unfortunately, it was too late. The boys from that villa were being led up the street in two tight rows surrounded by guards every few feet. Even under the best circumstances, there was no way I could get Wendell out of it. At least not then. I let out a slow breath and turned away. A few townspeople were standing nearby watching the procession. This time there was no cheering.

Exhausted, I trekked back to the villa and used every bit of strength I had to get through the brush and climb over my courtyard. The palms of my hands were cut and raw and my clothes were a mess.

I didn't think anyone had seen me slip back to my room. I was wrong. A soft knock on the archway, followed by a slave girl entering with a vase of water and some cloths, indicated otherwise. I had no idea if this was the morning "wake-up call" or if she was helping me guard my secret. All I could do was nod and smile.

By the time I wiped the dirt off of me, my palms had stopped bleeding and I was intact. I wish the same could have been said about my clothes. They looked like something my brother would have tossed into the wash expecting the machine to miraculously mend all the rips and tears. As I stood near the archway debating what to do next, the slave girl returned, this time with a handful of clothing.

I was flabbergasted. I had to stop myself from rushing over and giving her a hug. I reached for her hand, gave it a quick squeeze, and smiled. She helped me get dressed, applied some strange fragrant oil on my head and styled my hair into thin braids woven with ribbon. Wordless, she accompanied me down the corridor and back to the large dining room where I feasted the day before. A few other girls had already arrived, sitting comfortably on cushions, eating breads and cheeses.

One of them passed me a plate and I accepted as I sat down. I honestly didn't know how long

I could keep up this pretense. They were either going to think I was mute, or worse yet, they'd figure out that I was an imposter. I chewed my food very slowly so I wouldn't have to speak. Then, I did what every aspiring actress would do—I studied my lines. I listened to everything they said, watched their hand gestures, and repeated the words to myself.

I was about to say something when all of sudden the other girls in our entourage burst into the room giggling and laughing. They had no intention of sitting down to eat and motioned for us to join them. If it were under any other circumstances I would have listened to an expression my mother had drilled into my head since middle school. *Don't go off mindlessly following the crowd. Ha! Not much choice here, Mom. Don't worry. It's not like I'll be calling you any time soon to pick me up from some police station.*

A quick sip of some fruit juice and I was shoulder to shoulder with them. If I wanted to speak, I wouldn't have been heard due to their shrieking. For a minute, it almost felt as if I was back in middle school chasing after the football team. In a flash, it hit me. That's exactly what we were going to do. Girls that age don't get all that worked up over shopping or sightseeing. There's only one thing that would quicken a pulse, make a heart race, and send every hormone into overdrive—boys! Boys that these girls wanted to impress.

For me, there was only one boy on my mind and I didn't need to impress him. I needed to save his sorry little butt, or at the very least, give it a good whack!

Chapter Twenty-nine:

Wendell

Blood dance. I'm sure that's what he said. Not *blood bath* or *bludgeon,* but *blood dance.* I kept repeating the words to myself the entire way back to our villa. I was counting on Yidini and Sima to tell me what that was as soon as we were alone. With the guards breathing down our necks as we walked, there was no way to hold a conversation.

Blood dance. It had to be some sort of ritual involving red capes and fancy footwork around the bulls. How bad could that be? Then again, it might involve some acrobatics with red banners kind of like an over-the-top color guard routine for some big city band. I mean, one of the words was *dance,* wasn't it?

"No, no, not people dancing," Yidini said as he helped himself to a piece of sweet bread once we were back in our room. "It's not the people who dance; it's the blood as it spills to the ground."

"Blood?" I shouted out. "Who's blood? You mean I have to kill a bull?"

Sima tried not to laugh as Yidini explained it to me.

"No, it's not the bull that gets killed, it's the jumper if he isn't strong enough to lift himself over the animal's head while they stand face to face. It is not the same as the running jump over the bull. That is much easier."

Much easier? Were these people all insane? I could barely get over that bull in the arena. The only reason I did was because the thing lifted me up with his big head.

I tried to keep my voice from cracking as I spoke.

"So what do I do?"

"You approach the bull, look him in the eye and grab onto his horns. Then you push yourself up, bend your head down, lean forward and lift your legs above your head so that you tumble over the bull."

If there was any color in my face, it was gone. I knew exactly what they wanted me to do- a high bar somersault, using the bull's horns instead of a bar. Geez, I didn't think I had enough muscle strength to get my feet off the ground, let alone my body. I had to figure a way out of it.

"The red cloth. It means *blood dance,*" I said as Yidini continued to eat. "What does the blue cloth mean?"

"Water ride."

Water ride. That sounded a heck of lot nicer. Immediately I had images of some ancient form of water skiing or boat races.

"What do you and Sima have to do for it?"

"We must ride on the backs of the big fish as they jump into the air."

"Is that all?"

"No, sometimes the fish toss riders up in the air and they must dive back into the water. They cannot allow themselves to fall in as if they were a rock."

This was really unfair. The one thing I probably could have done without breaking my neck was the dolphin ride. Maybe Yidini or Sima would switch cloths with me.

I held out my red cloth and looked at them but before I could say anything, Sima spoke.

"Once you have been given a cloth, you cannot change it. It is a great honor to receive the red cloth. It means you will be in the final contest. Yidini and I have yet to prove ourselves. Only the very best sea riders are chosen for the final competition. You have already been selected."

Terrific. Do not pass GO. Do not collect $200. Head right on over to the blood bath.

I didn't feel like eating much that night. I was too exhausted and too petrified to think about what the next day would be like. Getting to sleep wasn't much better. Every time I closed my eyes all I could see were giant horns aiming straight for my chest.

Chapter Thirty:

Kitane

At first it looked like angry waters splashing up from the sea, but as we got closer, I saw it was dolphins jumping so high out of the water that their entire bodies glistened in the sunlight. The shoreline was filled with people waving and watching.

My mother approached me and spoke softly.

"It's the *water ride.* Watch carefully, Kitane. The boys will be swimming out to ride the beasts."

"I don't remember this from last year," I said, unable to take my eyes off of the giant creatures.

"That's because it is not part of the arena. The *water ride* is used to select a few choice champions who will compete in the Taurokathapsia."

I tried to count the number of swimmers I could see.

"Are those all of the boys, mother?"

"No, not all. Certain boys, who have demonstrated particular skills with the bulls, do not need to compete in the water. They go directly to the arena."

Our boat turned towards the harbor and its long line of docks so I could no longer watch the boys as they were tossed into the water by the dolphins. The thought that one of them might be chosen as my prospective husband gave me knots in my stomach. The only good news was that Mother hovered over her personal slaves the minute we reached the shore. I could hear her directing them to be careful with her belongings. Wasting no time, I had a quick conversation with one of the oarsmen.

I made it clear that I would generously reward whoever located the demon girl and got word to me before informing Father. I knew he had sent ships to look for her. I also knew that word travels faster than any sea going vessel. By nightfall, I expected that oarsman to have spread the word among his men. Some of them would be rowing on other ships. Bigger ships.

A generous reward from me was bound to carry more weight than a dictate from my father. Mother was still preoccupied with her clothing and didn't notice that I had directed my slave to search through the marketplaces and streets for that demon girl.

The slave I selected was quick on her feet and familiar with Thera. She had been there before and knew exactly where we would be staying. I made our conversation brief.

"Be discrete but firm. Try to find out if anyone has seen that girl. Get as much information as you can and hurry. You need to be at the villa where I am staying before it gets dark."

She nodded and took off from the dock quickly, disappearing into the crowd that had gathered by the boats. I feigned a sudden interest in Mother's clothing and rushed over to her.

"I hope the slaves haven't forgotten anything, Mother," I said as she motioned for our litter to be loaded.

"Everything is in order, Kitane. I've seen to it that all of our things will be taken directly to the villa. Come on, get inside. It's getting hot and I need to relax."

As our litter was carried from the docks through the streets, I glanced back toward the beach. In the distance I could hear the laughter of the girls who had gathered there. I was certain that they were the very ones with whom I would be sharing my lodging. The laughter turned to shrieking as I allowed myself one last look. Either they were anxious about being betrothed to a champion or they had no idea what their fathers had intended for them.

The marketplace seemed to stretch endlessly, blending into streets and alleys. Unlike Akrotiri, it wasn't limited to the square surrounding the harbor. I felt badly for the slaves who had to carry our litter uphill. At least there were only two of us, with Father arriving separately.

I recognized the villa the moment I caught a glimpse of it as our litter rounded a curve on the long street. The building was much larger than our home and had two full stories of rooms. As soon as we reached the front entrance, Mother spoke.

"The villa's house slaves will take our things inside and bring us refreshments in our quarters. Make sure your girl unpacks your things neatly. I will see you later this evening after we have dined."

"Won't we be eating together?" I asked.

"No. As I said earlier, you will be quartered with girls who have come of age. You will dine with them and attend all of the activities that they do. The night preceding the opening ceremony of the Taurokathapsia will be a grand banquet. You will be introduced to our hosts and I will see you at that time. And remember, Kitane, it is your choice. Follow your father's wishes or be sold."

She turned away from me and walked quickly through a large courtyard, accompanied by her slaves and a few from our host. I let out a sigh as I watched her disappear through a rounded archway. The slave girl standing near me must have heard her and asked me if I was all right. "I will be," I replied, finishing the rest of the sentence under my breath as she turned to help gather our belongings. ". . . once I sneak out of here and start looking for that demon girl myself."

Chapter Thirty-one:

Aeden

It was a downhill jog through the streets and past the marketplace. The momentum seemed to grow the closer we got to the harbor, and I could see the tall glass orb keeping watch on its city. The girls were chattering noisily, occasionally bursting out in uncontrollable giggles. As if on cue, I joined them. The breeze from the sea made our skirts lift up, causing even more peals of laughter.

We passed the docks and joined a small crowd of people who had gathered on the beach. I looked at the waters to see what the fuss was all about but all I saw was a large boat headed toward the harbor. I spun around and that's when I saw what had excited the girls to such extremes. Boys! At least a dozen or more. My instincts had been right. I stood there, open- mouthed as I watched them walk across the sand towards the water.

A contingent of guards blocked us from getting any closer. Wendell! He had to be among them. I moved back and forth straining to get a better look. Unfortunately, the boys faced the water and it was impossible to see their faces. With few exceptions, they all seemed to have the same build as Wendell Tyler Banton.

I wove in and out of the crowd, which had now grown to larger proportions. Apparently, this was quite the event. By now, the boys were all in the water swimming further and further away from the shore. Suddenly, I heard a giant splash and looked to see an enormous dolphin leaping straight up from the sea. Before I had time to think, another dolphin leapt into the air, and then a third. Within minutes, the entire area was filled with them. I wondered if the ones that Wendell and I had encountered on our inland trek were now part of this show.

My eyes widened as I continued to watch. One of the dolphins jumped so high that his entire body left the water. Something caught in my throat. The dolphin had a rider. The boy held on as the giant sea creature arched in the air before returning both of them to the sea. *Wendell? Was he the rider? This would be right up his alley.* I couldn't take my eyes off of what I was seeing. More and more boys were riding those dolphins and they weren't just hanging on.

They were getting tossed high into the air and had to dive back into the waters. The boys had to straddle those dolphins from the front of their fins so that the creatures could literally push them off. I knew Wendell could swim, but this? He'd be slammed back so hard in the water that he'd drown.

My hands began to tremble as I stood by helplessly, my eyes fixed on the waters. Meanwhile, the girls continued to laugh and shriek, oblivious to any danger for the riders. I had no idea how long I would be compelled to watch this spectacle. Then, just as quickly as it started, it ceased. In an instant the dolphins disappeared from view and the swimmers started to return to shore. No casualties. No one drowned. The boys were met by slaves who handed them towels and proceeded to help them dry.

I scanned the ranks for Wendell while I watched one of the guards count the number of boys. The centurion gave a nod of approval as the dolphin riders formed two lines and walked past us back to the city. I had a front seat view this time and studied each and every one of the swimmers. The girls who were with me, were also doing the same thing, all the while continuing their giggling.

Thirteen boys had passed me and no sign of Wendell. Could he have drowned without anyone knowing it? My stomach started to turn as the last few boys walked by. This couldn't be right. They couldn't have narrowed their "playing field" to only a dozen or so. I turned back to the girls and got my answer.

One of them made a face as the boys walked down the beach. The girl standing next to her tapped her on the shoulder, pointed, and gave a gesture to indicate that it was only half of the contenders. Half! Wendell was competing all right but not in the water. Without wasting a second, I made a beeline towards the arena and thanked my lucky stars that some hand gestures were universal in time and space.

Chapter Thirty-two:

Wendell

No soft music. No gentle lightening. Yidini, Sima, and I woke up to the sound of someone pounding on our archway. Seconds later, the slaves arrived with wash cloths and basins of water. I wasn't quick enough getting out of my cot and next thing I knew, one of them started to clean my feet. It tickled like crazy and I immediately jumped up.

Another slave rushed in carrying a large platter of fruits and dried fish. He set it down next to the cups that had been filled with juice. My mouth was as dry as a cactus and I'm sure it smelled like someone's armpit. I tried swishing the juice around to get that awful taste out of it. The slave noticed what I was doing and handed me some sort of a leaf.

A quick whiff and I knew it was mint. *No Colgate, Crest or Aquafresh toothpaste today, all we have on special are leaves.* I chewed it and spit it out but at least my breath was bearable.

"May the gods be with you, Widina," Yidini said as he changed into the clean clothing. "Sima and I will pray that you are returned safely tonight."

Terrific. They get to go on some fun-filled water adventure and I get to figure out how to stop a bull from goring me to death.

"Thank-you," I muttered. "You, too."

Another knock on the archway. This time it was a different slave waving a blue cloth. Time for my roommates to go off and have fun. I followed them into the corridor and watched as they headed towards the large courtyard. *You can try to escape now, Wendell. No one is looking. Go the other way. Find a window. Find a doorway. Find a . . .*

I took off faster than the time I had broken Aunt Eleanor's favorite crystal bird. Past the small courtyard, through the atrium, and out to the garden. My heart was pounding and I swear, I couldn't even feel my legs. I ran headfirst towards the walkway when the sound of a cymbal gave me such a jolt that my whole body shook. In that instant, I turned around to see where the noise came from and who made it. I was met face to face with one of the guards who happened to be leading the doomed red-cloth carrying guys like me to their certain deaths.

Crap. The only thing I could do was lie.

"I thought I was late," I said, forcing a smile. I'd been through this kind of dialogue before. Mostly with the dean of students and school principals. It was a solid routine I had mastered. *Yeah, too bad detention isn't what you're going to get.*

"Save your enthusiasm for the arena," was the guard's response as he pointed to my place in line. Two by two we walked through the garden, down the long narrow steps and onto the street. From there, it was uphill to the arena. Our slaves followed behind and I actually began to wonder if I could trade places with one of them.

I knew we were almost there by the rancid smell that went up my nose. It was the bulls. Or their manure. Or both. The stench got stronger the closer we got and by the time we had reached the building I felt like gagging. The bulls were separated into four corrals and we were divided up evenly—five of us to each one. This time they didn't bother to sort us by height.

The bulls weren't sorted either. They were all about the same size. Not particularly large but far from being small. And they were in a stinking rotten mood. Same as the last time—kicking their hooves on the sand, snorting and making the worst noises possible.

Maybe they weren't too thrilled with the whole ordeal themselves. I was just starting to feel a bit relieved that none of the bulls was overly large or aggressive when something caught my eye. Behind the corrals I could see a few men trying to lead three gigunda white and brown bulls to another corral. I wanted to toss up my breakfast, lunch, and any meal I had eaten in the past month!

You're as good as dead, Wendell. Guess what's coming?

There was no way I could convince myself that those bulls weren't meant for me. The smaller ones were the starting act and I was part of the main show.

The morning was brutal. Yidini and Sima were right. The men in the arena lead the small bulls to the ring and showed us what we were expected to do. It was a high bar somersault just as they described it. Except they forgot one thing—no do-overs. If I tried to escape I knew the guards would send a bull tearing after me. If I tried to grab onto the bull's horns and wasn't quick enough, the bull would come tearing after me. Either way, I was dead meat.

Run and get killed. Grab horns and get killed. I needed another option and I needed it fast. The other boys in my group had already mastered the art of tumbling over the bull and it was my turn. I unlatched the gate and walked across the hard packed sand towards the bull. I was just a few feet away when out of nowhere, this crazy girl came rushing across the arena towards the guards.

Aeden? Could it possibly be her?

All I could see was long dark hair and some billowy skirt. I figured she found a change of clothing. The guard motioned for me to go back to the stall and wait. I paused and took my time. If she was up to something, I had to be ready. I knew she didn't know the language but heck, that wasn't something that would stop her.

I held my breath, not knowing what to expect.

Chapter Thirty-three:

Kitane

The musician had described the demon girl as wild and fiery when I went back to ask. He said I would know her by the way she moved. "Even her hair refuses to obey," he said. "And when the sunlight touches it, a few strands illuminate like gold." "And what about the *gift*?" I asked. "How will I recognize it?" "You won't. The *gift* appears quite ordinary in body. It is *where* and *how* the *gift* made its way to our city that makes it so coveted for the gods."

It didn't matter. If I found the demon girl, I would make sure she delivered the *gift* to me. I crept quietly and carefully down the corridor through a small courtyard and then an atrium. I could see the city past a large archway and hurried to the wall that surrounded the villa. The house slaves were busy unpacking my clothing, perfumes and jewelry. No one saw me lower myself from the wall to the bushes and trees that shielded the villa.

My personal slave would be in the marketplace by now, and I had to find her. If she had found out the whereabouts of the demon girl I would need to act quickly. If not, then the search would continue. I hurried down the streets keeping a guarded eye on the sun. I would have to return to the villa before it slipped out of sight.

The narrow road forked into two branches and I took the one with tight rows of whitewashed houses. It was past midday and the sun had reached its peak. I expected to see slaves working in the gardens but the street was empty. Maybe they had all gone to the market.

I kept walking, paying attention to the small alleyways that connected the larger streets. Still nothing. Ahead I could see another fork with the marketplace downhill to my left and the arena across a small knoll on the right. I had started to turn towards the marketplace when I saw someone dart through an alleyway in the direction of the arena. Her blue and red skirt caught my eye at first but as I lifted my head, I saw how the sunlight turned strands of her hair gold. I had never seen sunlight alter the color of anyone's dark hair before. I felt my pulse race and my heart pound. It was the demon girl!

The ground rushed towards me as I raced after her. She was fast. No matter how hard I pushed my legs to run, I couldn't keep up with her. It didn't matter. I knew where she was going. It had to be the arena. Had she hidden the *gift* there? The musician said that the *gift* looked no different from other boys his age. Only the demon girl would know who it was. I forced myself to run faster.

By the time I reached the large wooden gates to the arena, there was no sign of her. The guards who stood steadfast in front of the building had not seen her either.

"I know she is in here. I must speak to your captain. It is urgent. The gods will bring down their wrath upon Thera if we do not find this demon."

The centurions could see the fear in my eyes and knew that I was telling the truth. They opened the gates and I ran down a tight corridor that separated the corrals. I was so intent on talking to the captain that I was oblivious to the bull that had just been brought into the ring. I ran past it, narrowly missing one of the boys whose turn it was to jump it.

The guard motioned for the boy to stay put and grabbed me by the elbow, whisking me away from the ring. My words might have been garbled but my message wasn't. Within seconds the guard sounded an alert and the preparation ceased.

The demon girl was somewhere in the arena and its guards, slaves and bull masters were about to find her.

Chapter Thirty-four:

Wendell

Everything happened at once. One of the guards motioned for me to return to the gated area. *You don't have to ask me twice, buddy, I'm out of here!* As far as I was concerned, that bull could've stood there all day snorting and kicking his hooves.

Once I made sure that my blood wasn't about to "hip-hop" on the sand, I tried to get a better look at the girl. It wasn't Aeden. It was some nutcase who kept pointing and carrying on as if the world was about to end. Apparently, her performance worked because the next thing I knew, all of the guards and the bull masters started racing around the arena. Not only that, but they made the slaves dart around, too.

Last time I saw anything at all that remotely resembled this was when someone phoned my school about a suspicious package. What the heck were they looking for in the arena? The scariest things were the bulls and they didn't arrive in small boxes. I figured some sort of venomous snake got loose or worse.

We were told to "stay put" as the SWAT team of guards descended on the place like the seventeen year locusts. *"Stay Put." That was fine with me. I wasn't about to go running around.* The other four boys in my group had backed out of our small waiting area by the corrals and I was about to join them when I heard a noise above my head. It sounded like an insect on steroids.

"Psst! Psst!"

I looked up at the second story box seats above me. Nothing. The sound got louder. Then it got personal.

"PSST! Wendell!"

"Aeden? Miss Aeden?"

It was her all right; I recognized the voice even though I couldn't see her but I yelled back.

"Get out of here! Something escaped in here and the guards are trying to catch it."

"The only thing that should escape is you! What is taking you so long?"

"You think I can escape? Take a good look! Prison inmates at Leavenworth have a better chance of escaping."

"Can you make a run for it now?"

"What do you think? There are guards posted all over the place. Haven't you noticed?"

"I had to climb in from an outside trellis. I am serious, Wendell. You have *got* to escape. This is not what you think. I don't care how much fun you're having!"

"Fun? Fun? You call this fun? I'm waiting in line to be gored to death by a bull!"

Across from where I was standing, I could see guards, slaves and bull masters searching frantically for something. A few of them were headed my way. Aeden must have seen them too because the tone of her voice changed and she got quieter.

"When does this event start? The actual thing. Not your practices."

"Tomorrow night. But that's just some sort of pageant. The action is the day after tomorrow if I live that long."

"Okay. Fine. I'll figure out a way to get you out of there during the event. With such a big crowd, it should be easier."

"Are you still on the beach?"

"If I was still on the beach I would have sent that bull to gore you myself! No. I'm in a villa. They mistook me for someone from a royal or wealthy family."

By now the guards were only a few yards away. I pretended to clear my throat as I choked out the words, "Get Out."

If she said anything, I didn't hear her. Two of the boys from my group rushed back in to tell me that we were all being escorted back to the villa. Whatever got loose in the arena, I owed it my life for that day. Maybe if I was lucky, someone would bring their pet cobra tomorrow.

Chapter Thirty-five:

Aeden

That infuriating little jerk! He had no idea what they intended for him. If he did, he would have tried harder to escape. Now it was all left to me and I was clueless. It wasn't as if I could waltz myself over to those guards and say, "I'm sorry, but your next victim needs to get back to the 21st century."

I made sure no one could see me as I practically pasted myself to the floor of the arena seating box and stared through the wooden slats. Below me, guards were shouting orders and people were running all over. It was only a matter of time before they checked each upper floor box. What if Wendell was right and it was a snake? Vipers were fairly common on Santorini.

Don't make any sudden moves, Aeden. The thing could be coiled up in your little seating area. Moving my head slowly, I checked the floor on either side of me before inching my way to a corner of the box where I could see the entire compartment. All clear. Nothing. Time to make a run for it.

Keeping myself low to the ground, I started for the open arch across from the seating. It was a better alternative than using the stone stairwells. They would be thick with guards or slaves running about. I had managed to climb up the wooden trellis but climbing down was worse. No place to see where to put your feet. I would have to use one foot and move it around in order to find secure footing. The thing was meant for vines, not people. That was the other problem. I had to be really careful where to grab on.

The dark corridor that connected the seating boxes to the stairwells was clear. At least for the moment. My neck creaked as I stood up quickly and ran for the opening. Too late. Someone had reached the top of the stairs and had seen me. No time to think about footing or hand holds. What I did think about was a litany of words, all meant for Wendell, that could never be used in public.

I spun around, held tight to the ledge and anchored my right foot on the first solid thing I felt. Then, I did the same with the left foot. Above me, I could hear a girl's loud voice. No time to check for footing. It was Paris all over again, except no one was shooting at me. One more foothold and that was it. I pushed myself off the trellis, tucked my knees in and braced for a hard fall.

The sandy ground was softer than I expected and the "tuck and roll" I learned from having to do minor stunts on stage saved me from breaking any bones or getting cut. Without wasting a second, I took the first alleyway I saw and ran uphill, crisscrossing alleyways and streets until I was sure I wasn't being followed.

With the gold ribbon still securely fastened to my wrist, I felt certain the centurions would let me back inside the palatial villa. I walked quickly. It was getting to be late afternoon. Ahead of me, three alleyways converged, and tumbling out of one of them was the group of girls. They weren't as boisterous as before but were still loud enough to be heard from down the block.

I raced towards them, hoping to blend in inconspicuously. One of them immediately showed me a bracelet and some silks that I imagine she obtained at the marketplace. I practically gushed over them which resulted in more girls showing me their treasures. Before I knew it, we were back at the estate on the hill.

Only a bit of commotion at the gate. One of the girls in the rear of the group lost her gold ribbon and the centurion sent for the house master to vouch for her. I glanced at my wrist and made sure my knot was tight before continuing on to my room.

The slaves had delivered food to our quarters and the girls spent the evening running about from room to room showing off clothing and jewelry. I sank onto my cot, exhausted and worried. What if I couldn't find a way to get Wendell out of the arena?

My last thought as I closed my eyes for the night was that I would be bitten by a viper before I could ever reach the bullring.

Chapter Thirty-six:

Kitane

That demon girl's powers were strong. She was able to vanish through an archway as if she could walk on air. I was not the only one in awe of her darkness. One of the guards who had entered the corridor also saw her disappear through the opening. We were too late.

The captain assured me that everyone would be vigilant in their search to find her. She would most certainly be caught the moment she entered the arena for the Taurokathapsia. I thanked him and raced out of there, frantic that my slave had already returned to the villa and was looking for me.

I knew that I had to walk uphill. The winding alleys and wider streets would all lead to the palatial estate where we were staying. But some wove and twisted, forcing me back to the same place. It seemed like hours until I was certain I saw the road that led to the villa. I could hear voices coming from the other end and ran as quickly as I could to catch up.

It was a cluster of girls. Royal girls. Wealthy girls. Their ruffled skirts and colorful bodices stood out against the whitewashed houses. They had to be part of the entourage that would attend the grand event. Maybe one of them had spotted the demon girl. I moved quickly until I was only a few feet from the rear of the group. By then, we were at the front gates to the villa.

One by one, the girls waved their arms at the centurions and were welcomed inside. Not so for me. Mother had neglected to tell me that I would be given a token to indicate that I was a welcomed guest. Had the house slave arrived with my token only to find that I had gone? I cringed at the thought of her telling this to the slave master who would undoubtedly inform my mother.

I waited anxiously while the centurion sent for the house master. The gods protected me. They knew I sought out the demon girl so they, in turn, shielded me from my mother's wrath. She never knew that I had left the villa.

I fastened the knot tightly to my wrist and waved the gold ribbon, that the housemaster gave me, in the air. For a brief second, it reminded me of the color the demon girl's hair when the sun touched it.

Chapter Thirty-seven:

Wendell

Yidini and Sima were pacing back and forth in our room when I got back from that ordeal in the arena.

"You're alive!" they both shouted at once. Then, Yidini continued to speak. "I feared your blood was dancing on the sand. You weren't here when we returned. Was the bull jump terrible?"

"I never jumped. I never got near the bull."

"Then are you being expelled from the Taurokathapsia?" he asked.

"I don't think so. I don't think anyone even noticed that I didn't get a chance to jump the bull. There was a huge commotion in the arena and all the guards were looking for something. We were escorted back here."

I barely spit the last word out of my mouth when a guard knocked on our archway and stepped into the room. He handed Yidini and Sima red cloths like the one I got the day before.

I figured I would probably join their group and get to jump over a bull tomorrow. At least I'd live to see another night.

I was about to say something like "congratulations" when the guard handed me a cloth. This time it was a white one. *Holy crap! The color of surrender. Were they going to toss me out?* At least I could find Aeden and kiss this primitive civilization good-bye. I waited to see what the guard was going to do when all of a sudden Yidini and Sima started to congratulate me.

"The white cloth. The white cloth. You have been chosen to jump a white bull. You must be beaming with honor!" Sima shouted.

Beaming with honor? More like trying not to crap my pants.

I didn't know what to say. I stood there staring at the cloth. The guard turned away and headed down the corridor, probably to ruin some other kid's day. Without realizing it, I had almost crunched up the small piece of linen. Finally, I managed to say something.

"Weren't those white bulls the enormous ones with the really sharp horns?"

"Yes. The bulls of honor," Yidini replied. "Only champions of the white bulls may fight to the death."

"Fight to the WHAT?"

My voice had reached a high pitch and I was one step away from losing it. Yidini looked at me as if he couldn't understand why I wasn't thrilled with my new found status.

"Champions of the white bulls fight each other to the death. The winners are rewarded by their betrothals to the daughters of the wealthiest families."

My God! This is insane! Death would be bad enough, but marriage? Marriage to some girl? I don't care how rich she is.

I tried to sound perfectly calm and normal.

"What if someone refuses to fight? What happens?"

"He is brought into the arena and all of the bulls are let loose to charge him. If he survives, he is free to leave Thera."

"Has anyone survived?"

"No. Never."

Stinkin' lousy choice. Fight to the death. Marriage. Death by stampede.

"You are so fortunate, Widina," Yidini went on, "Sima and I must prove ourselves tomorrow in the ring while you practice the skills of hand-to-hand combat."

"You mean I have to kill someone tomorrow, too?"

"No, only in the arena. Come, let us join the others and get something to eat."

I didn't feel like eating but went along anyway. When we were all seated on the cushions in the dining area, Yidini asked me about the commotion in the arena.

"Did you know what the guards were looking for?"

"No. Everything stopped at once and the slaves had to look, too."

"It was probably a viper," Sima cut in. "If a viper gets into the arena, it will panic the bulls and they could kill each other. No wonder the guards were as frantic as you said."

"We don't know that it was viper, Sima," Yidini said as he popped a small dried fish into his mouth. "It could have been something worse."

I shrugged my shoulders and asked.

"What? What could be worse?"

"There are rumors of a demon girl who came from Akrotiri. I heard talk of it today at the harbor."

"A demon girl? I don't understand."

"She is said to have helped a special sacrificial gift to escape. Her powers are tremendous."

Demon girl? Gift? Could this day get any worse? As if death and marriage weren't enough...

I started to put an apricot into my mouth when everything made sense at once.

Holy hell! It wasn't a darn viper. It had to have been Aeden! Aeden was the one in the arena who freaked them out.

I nearly choked on the pit when I realized that we might never get out of here.

Chapter Thirty-eight:

Aeden

If you took the preparations that Great Britain's royal family made for their weddings, combined them with Cinderella's step sisters and added every prom since 1950, it wouldn't hold up to what it was like getting ready for this event. From what I could piece together from Wendell, there was apparently some sort of pageant or parade. Then again, his command of Ancient Greek wasn't exactly on target.

When I awoke the next morning, not only was a house slave there to help me wash, but a second one arrived to clean each and every one of my toes carefully. For once in my life I was thankful that I had been too busy with rehearsals to schedule a pedicure or she would have fainted at the bright polish I usually wear.

I joined the other girls in the atrium for our morning meal—dried fish, breads, cheeses and fruits. When we finished, we were all ushered into a special room where the slaves had laid out everyone's attire for the evening. Everyone's except mine.

Time to play charades again, Aeden. Give an award winning performance, too, while you're at it.

Shrugging my shoulders, pacing back and forth, and finally bursting into sobs that my sophomore theater coach would have been proud of, I acted as if the worst crime had been committed—someone lost my "gown for the ball."

Immediately the slaves pointed fingers at each other and raced out of there to see where the missing clothing was. In the meantime, I let a few of the girls console me as I wiped away crocodile tears.

Next thing I knew, the house mistress arrived with an armload of the most dazzling fabrics I had ever seen. She snapped her fingers and a young, lithe slave held out the clothing in front of me and began to take measurements using a string as if it was a measuring tape.

In an instant, she and the fabric were gone. The house mistress said something to me and I responded by nodding and offering a slight smile.

Way to go, Cinderella!

The mid part of the day was spent playing some sort of board game that resembled

Parcheesi. I caught on quickly and moved the white cylinder across the mosaic board as if I had done this thousands of times before.

By early afternoon, I was presented with the most lavish skirt and bodice that I had ever seen. The seamstress helped me try it on and astounded me by fastening two long gold necklaces around my neck. Satisfied that I was ready for the evening, she folded the clothing and placed it on one of the small tables in my room.

We were served a lighter meal consisting of some sort of yogurt with fruits and berries. Then, one by one, we were led into brightly painted bathing rooms that had large red and gold bathtubs in the corners. As I walked down the corridor of the bathing area, I looked at each of the rooms and gasped. It was unbelievable. Maybe Wendell was disappointed that he hadn't found a technologically savvy Atlantis, but I was in awe of how advanced this civilization really was. Until I started thinking about their penchant for human sacrifice and their taste for entertainment.

A few slave girls carried jugs of hot water to fill the bath so that I could immerse myself. It was the first time that I really felt clean since we slipped back in time. My back was scrubbed with a loofah and my hair was washed in fragrant oils.

Expecting to be dried off and ready to be

dressed, I stepped out of the tub and reached for one of the linen towels. The house slave immediately started to pat me dry and motioned for me to take a seat on one of the clay stools in the bathing area.

For the next hour, she and another slave worked on my hair as if I was about to be judged in some sort of beauty contest. Apparently they were not satisfied with the color. *I know. I know. I should have scheduled a salon appointment but how the heck did I know I'd wind up here.*

A mixture of black powder was applied to my hair and toweled dry. Then, more oils. They swept up part of my hair and embellished it with gold, yellow and red ribbon. They curled the other strands by twisting them over some sort of dowels. Finally, they styled the front and let me put back the earrings that I had taken off when I first stepped into the tub.

Wrapped in a large linen towel, I followed the slaves to another room where the girls were busy applying make-up. Finally! Something I could excel at! Four years of theater study and numerous classes on stage make-up actually paid off!

I was good with greasepaint. Great with spirit gum. Terrific with powders and wonderful with all sorts of glosses. What I saw instead was something even easier—minerals! Little jars of greyish black minerals, silvery green minerals, and reddish minerals were ready for the taking.

I knew that the Ancient Greeks, Babylonians and Egyptians all used kohl to line their eyes and iron oxide for their lips. The silvery green mineral had to be eye shadow. I was back in my own turf. In less than twenty minutes I had transformed myself into the epitome of Minoan beauty. Not bad considering the only mirror I had was made of polished metal.

As I set the round mirror back on its table, a girl tapped my arm, held out one of the jars and said something as she pointed to her face. That small gesture of hers was the start of my afternoon as a make-up artist for no less than eight of the girls. By the time I had applied the last bit of greenish powder to an eyelid, the slaves were escorting us to our rooms.

The sun had started to go down when my house slave arrived to help me dress. Up until now I had managed to communicate by merely repeating a few phrases. I cringed at the thought of being asked something tonight that required a lengthy explanation. How would I fake it?

You spent four years majoring in theater! You mean you can't think of anything? Faint! Scream! Choke! Point and run! Laugh! Act appalled! Don't expect a career in acting if you can't manage one little performance.

In the corridor outside my room, the girls were already gathering and giggling. All I had to do was let them do the talking.

Chapter Thirty-nine:

Kitane

What a total waste of a day! Preening, primping, and fussing. The last thing I wanted to do was to have my body cleansed, make-up applied, and hair styled before getting into some elaborately fashioned outfit. I needed to be in the city looking for that demon girl. Instead, I was forced to send my personal slave, Ariadnh, with explicit instructions to check the area surrounding the arena.

I knew Mother would be more than displeased if my make-up wasn't applied properly or if my hair didn't reflect my status. Without Ariadnh to take care of those tasks, I was left in a quandary— ask assistance from one of the house slaves or try to do it myself. As fate would have it, one of the other royal girls knew how to apply the tints and powders perfectly. At first I found it strange since that is a skill left to personal slaves. Then I realized that these girls have come from other lands where it may indeed be common practice for them.

After watching the girl use the most subtle of shades to enhance the blandest features on three others, I approached her and asked her if she would apply my make-up. The girl simply nodded as she dipped her finger into the luminescent powder. I tried to speak with her but she motioned for me to be still. I imagine it was because she needed to concentrate. When she finally held out the mirror to me to inspect my image, I was stunned. Never in my life did my features radiate in such a way.

The house slaves were familiar with hair styling, and by the end of the day, I knew Mother would be pleased. I wanted to thank the girl with the dark powdery hair but I did not get a chance. We had to return to our rooms in order to get dressed for the evening. Luckily, Ariadnh had raced back from the marketplace in time to help me prepare. Unfortunately, she was unable to find the demon girl and I was fast becoming distraught.

The banquet was held in the four large rooms that surrounded a garden atrium. We dined on sea delicacies and roasted goat, washing it down with grape and pomegranate wine. I told a few of the girls about the horrific demon girl and her powers. No one had seen anyone who resembled her.

Mother had me escorted from my room before the banquet to introduce me to our hosts and inform me that Father had arrived from Akrotiri. He was not successful in his endeavor to retrieve the *gift*. That meant I still had time. The Taurokathapsia would last three days. Maybe in that time my boat captain would have good news.

When the sun had finally set and the first star of the night appeared, we were led out of the atrium and up a long staircase that took us to a rooftop garden. Peering over the long balcony we watched as the Taurokathapsia procession began. Thera's beacon orb illuminated the harbor and cast a reddish glow in the dark.

From the villa near the arena, the contenders marched in unison, their torches held high as they approached the shore. Like a coiling snake, they wound through the narrow streets until at last they fanned out onto the docks. At once, the cymbals clanged and the boys remained motionless. The ceremony master held two giant torches in the air and waved them across his body, signaling the start of the Taurokathapsia. We were too far away to hear the shouts and shrieks from the people who had gathered around them.

From my vantage point on the roof, I watched as the contenders fanned out further until their torches formed the shape of a bull's head. Another clang of cymbals and they were back in their processional line weaving through the city until the last of them entered their villa for the night.

All around me, the girls were buzzing with an excitement that I could not feel. Only the one who had applied my make-up seemed subdued. Was she being forced into an unwanted marriage as well? I had to ask her. If I was right and she was facing a similar fate as mine, then perhaps we could work together to catch the demon girl.

<h1 style="text-align:center">Chapter Forty:</h1>

<h1 style="text-align:center">Wendell</h1>

It was official. I was now participating in the *March of the Zombies* as we were each draped in a tunic over our loincloths and given a torch to carry as soon as it got dark. I felt like a zombie, too. Tired. Worn-out. Knuckles and fingers scabbing over with dried blood. Hell of a day.

It started the usual way with a guard pounding on our archway and slaves hurrying in to wash us and give us something to eat. Heck, even the Marriott, Hilton and Hampton couldn't touch that kind of hospitality.

Red cloths were called out first and lined up. White cloths followed. We all went to the arena. Only difference was that Yidini, Sima and the others in their group were taken to some dusty corrals in front while my tribe got to scope out four large rounded platforms that were about a foot or two off the ground.

The guards motioned for us to stand under

the canopies of the arena and wait. *What now? A giant bull? A colossal beast that you've been harboring for the past month? What?*

Suddenly I remembered my conversation with the roommates. No bulls. No beast. Fighting each other to the death in hand-to-hand combat. Maybe if I was lucky, I'd upchuck my breakfast and they'd let me sit this one out.

As I looked around me, I realized that I was the only one who wasn't all pumped up about the prospect of knocking someone's teeth out. Yeah, I was in junior boxing league back in Connecticut but we wore really thick gloves and we didn't kill each other. The air whistled out of my nostrils while I stood there waiting. Finally, three slaves arrived who were carrying thick leather straps. *Oh terrific. Maybe the guards will whip the daylights out of us first.*

I stepped back, not knowing what to expect when I was asked to hold out my hands. I fidgeted instead, looking around at what was going to happen to the other guys. They couldn't wait to hold out their hands. *Are you all insane?* I braced myself, expecting to see someone get a bloody lashing. Instead, the slaves wrapped the guy's hands in the leather straps and I let out a slow breath. We weren't about to be whipped after all. The leather straps were our handwraps.

Okay. Maybe this wasn't going to be so bad

after all. Yidini did say that no one gets killed in practice. That particular feature of the event would be reserved for one of the three days starting tomorrow. Lucky me. And lucky me again, because I wasn't in the first group of boxers. It gave me time to watch what they were doing.

No surprises. Same stuff I was used to. Jabs, cross, hook and uppercut for offense. Slip and turn, block, and cover-up for defense. I didn't see any clinching where the guys got so close that a punch couldn't be thrown, but that didn't mean it couldn't or wouldn't happen.

Next thing I knew, it was my turn. My turn with a kid who was my size. *No death match today.* We jabbed, crossed, hooked and went at each other for what seemed like an eternity. *Haven't these guys heard of three minute rounds?* We also blocked, covered and slipped until we were both exhausted. Finally one of the referees (guards with an attitude) called a stop to our fighting fiasco and sent us back to stand under the canopy. Slaves brought us water as we watched the other kids duke it out. More than a few of them were worse than we were. Not a good sign. We'd be pitted up against stronger guys. That never happened in junior boxing league because someone's mother always complained. *Well, no mothers here today. Take your chances Dell T.*

I guzzled down the water and watched the fighting in front of me. This was one time when I wished I didn't have front row seats. The victors emerged all right and they were brutal. Bigger. Faster. Motivated. I suppose I was motivated, too. Especially when I considered "going the distance" meant "don't get your sorry butt killed."

Sure enough, I was called to the front again. This came after a feeble attempt of trying to get excused to find a bathroom. The guard pointed to a corner by the corrals and couldn't understand why I didn't want to pee on the ground like a bull. In the end, I peed on the ground, taking my time in the hopes that they would find someone else to spar with the Godzilla who was waiting for me. They didn't.

What I lacked in actual skills I made up for with fancy footwork and a powerful straight punch that came out of nowhere and knocked the guy to the ground. He staggered and wobbled. I looked around half expecting these maniacs to send in someone else to replace him but they didn't. Instead, the arena master handed me a gold cloth and held up three fingers high in the air for everyone to see. *Three what? Bulls tomorrow? Dried fish on my plate for dinner? Girls who would marry me? Or worse yet, three more fights.*

Dehydrated and queasy, I joined the other winners and losers under the canopy until it was time for us to be escorted back to the villa. Yidini and Sima had it easy. All they had to do was jump over small bulls. I couldn't wait to ask them what *three* meant as soon as we were back in the room.

"The gold cloth? The gold cloth *and* the number three?" Yidini could hardly contain himself and Sima just kept muttering, "gold cloth" over and over again. It was starting to freak me out.

"What? What does this mean? Am I expected to kill three bulls or three people tomorrow?"

Both of them laughed and tried to explain at once before Yidini took over.

"It is the order of the Taurokathapsia. There are three events, one for each of the three days. The champions who receive the gold cloth *and* the number three are honored to participate in all of the contests. You should be elated."

Elated? I was scared out of my gourd! What if Aeden couldn't come up with a plan? Then what?

I tried not to picture myself getting gored to death, punched to death or trampled to death. It wasn't easy. While Yidini and Sima were stuffing themselves with some sort of roasted meat and bread, I was trying keep the earlier contents of my stomach from coming up in my mouth.

The sun was slowly setting in the sky and I was absolutely drained. Nervous or not, all I wanted to do was sleep. Ha! As I walked to my cot, someone banged on the archway door loud enough to set the food platters shaking. It was one of the guards.

We had a few minutes for our slaves to clean us up and get us ready for some sort of parade. As soon as it got dark, we were lined up in single file in the corridor, given a heavy lit torch, and directed to follow the person in front of us.

Seriously? I could barely hang on to that torch. Half the time I thought I was going to set fire to the hair on the guy's head in front of me. It took both of my arms to hold the darn thing as we went out the villa gates, down the street, across smaller streets and all over hell's creation and back before standing perfectly still on one of the docks in the harbor. Talk about freaking nightmares, this was it! To top it off, I swear they installed some sort of reddish strobe light near the docks. If the fighting and marching didn't give me a headache, that stupid orb would. *When is this going to end?*

Guess what? We had to do the same thing over again on the way home. What the heck kind of parade was that? Other than someone clanging the cymbals when we got to the harbor, there was no music, no dancing, no food, no nothing.

I fell headfirst onto my cot and didn't wake up until I heard the familiar pounding on the archway.

Chapter Forty-one:

Aeden

Even standing outside on the rooftop I could smell the heavy scented perfumes that the girls were wearing. We watched the processional of torch lights heading to the harbor and I wondered which one was Wendell. It was spellbinding as they snaked their way through the streets. Wendell wouldn't see it that way and for a split second I almost felt sorry for him. *Almost.* He was the one who got us into this mess.

One of the girls whose make-up I applied walked over to me and said something. I pretended that I couldn't hear her with everyone else talking so she motioned for me to move to a more secluded spot. I was trapped and didn't want to call attention to myself. I followed her to the corner of the roof that gave us a wide angled view of the city and the harbor.

She kept her voice low and leaned in as she spoke. I had absolutely no idea what she was saying but from the way she was speaking, I knew she wasn't sharing gossip. Up until now I had managed to keep a low profile and just repeat what people were saying. I also caught on that the word "nai" meant "yes." The girl continued to whisper and then waited for my response. I nodded slowly, repeated the last few words she said and then added "nai."

Whatever it was, I knew she was not asking me to style her hair, do her make-up or pick out her clothing. From the way she gestured, she might have been looking for someone. It wasn't until the "nai" slipped from my lips more than once that I had the unsettling feeling she was including me in something sinister or dangerous. *Too late to change your mind, Aeden. You already said yes!*

The girl gave my hand a quick squeeze and walked back to the crowd in time to see the procession fan out across the docks. I stared straight ahead, mesmerized by the sight in front of me. The image of a giant bull's head took up the entire harbor. Poor Wendell. The Ceremony of the Bulls was about to begin.

Wendell had said that he thought it lasted three days. I wasn't sure he'd make it through the first one. That night, as I tossed and turned on my cot, I tried to think of some way to get him out of it. I told him that it would be easier with a big crowd. Lots of action. Lots of diversions. Surely I'd figure out some way to sneak him out of there when no one was looking.

Then there was the girl who asked me to do something. How would *that* figure into the scheme of things? Only one thing was certain. I didn't have three days. I had one. And I didn't have an idea in my head.

Chapter Forty-two:

Wendell

Dried fish and yogurt for breakfast. No way to file a complaint with the culinary staff. It wouldn't matter. It wasn't as if I was going to be alive for another meal. The morning was spent with what I'd like to call "special grooming and bathing." I had only witnessed this type of production once in my life and that was when we had to take Aunt Eleanor's bichon to the doggie spa.

First, a short stocky slave inspected my toenails and fingernails. Then, he proceeded to dip them in some oily stuff and then clip them with a primitive knife. *Clipping the dog's nails—$12.00.* Next, I was taken to a small room that had paintings of dolphins on the walls and a large oval bathtub off to the side. Before I could protest, I was escorted by two washroom slaves into the tub. That's right, two slaves. One to keep bringing steaming hot water and the other to scrub my back with something that should have stayed at the bottom of the sea. *Bathing the dog— $25.00.*

When they were done, they each grabbed an arm and stood me up for the towel drying. *Fluff and dry—$8.00.* It was an ordeal I'd rather forget. They combed my hair, put sweet smelling oil on it and then twisted the top of it into little curls that they secured with long pins. *Great going guys! Are you going to put a ribbon and bow around my neck, too?*

Okay. So I didn't have to wear something ridiculous around my neck, but I did have to put on this elaborate loincloth with gold fringes and red, blue and yellow stripes. It looked like a circus tent with a flap opening up for the whole world to see the entertainment. When the slaves weren't looking, I took one of the pins from my head and used it to keep the flap from opening.

Yidini and Sima had already been "prepared" for the event and were waiting for me in the corridor near the courtyard with eight or nine other boys. I sat down on one of the stone benches and watched as more and more "carefully groomed victims" joined us. Off to the side, four large guards kept watch on us as if they expected one of us to make a break for it.

A few minutes later we were all lined up and the Bataan Death March began. Out the villa gates and uphill to the arena we walked.

Silently. Slowly. Carrying heavy banners since it wasn't enough torture just to walk uphill. Was this how Louis XVI felt when they led him to the guillotine? At least he didn't have to suffer with a last meal of dead fish. I tried to stay positive but all I could see were the horns of some pissed off bull coming straight at my chest.

The gold cloth and the number three. How much luckier could I get?

Chapter Forty-three:

Kitane

I was right. That girl who applied my make-up was being forced into a marriage that she didn't want. Same as me. When I told her about the demon girl and the *gift* she agreed to help me. Even though she knew it would anger the gods. She must have reasoned that the gods would retaliate, thus putting a hold on any betrothals. I could see her smile as I revealed my plan.

There was only one reason that the demon girl was in the arena. She had made sure that the *gift* was one of the contenders. But who? The musician said there was no way to tell. No use trying to guess which dark-haired bull-jumping fist-fighting champion stood between my happiness and my father's. It was the demon girl we had to find. Without her, my father's men would never be able to obtain the *gift*.

Killing the demon girl was one way to ensure that I would remain chaste and single.

The *gift* would go free. That is, if he survived the Taurokathapsia. While the other girls in the villa laughed and giggled throughout the banquet and the procession, I agonized over what would happen to me if I succeeded in killing her or having her killed. The answer frightened me more than I thought possible. *She would send other demon girls to torture my dreams and paralyze my thoughts.* No, I couldn't kill her. But I *could* render her unconscious for three days and nights.

The priceless spice that I had taken from the kitchen would buy the tiniest of vipers from the right seller. Ariadnh would need to scour the marketplace to find out who harbored such a thing and then proceed to make the trade. That meant she would not accompany me to the Taurokathapsia's opening day tomorrow. Mother would be furious and arrange to have her whipped, or worse yet, sold. I had to be careful. I had to make sure that I blended into the crowd of girls so as not to call attention to myself. Mother would never know that I went without my personal slave.

All I could hope to accomplish on opening day was to find out where the demon girl watched the events. Together with my new found accomplice, we would look for a girl whose hair danced like fire in the sun.

Chapter Forty-four:

Aeden

Another morning in "Cinderella's castle." This time there was a heightened intensity as the girls applied their make-up and waited for the house slaves to style their hair. By now I was familiar with the process and was able to work on two more girls while my own hair felt as if it would never breathe under all that black dye and oil.

The girl who spoke with me last night on the rooftop kept her voice barely above a whisper when she approached me. Whatever I had agreed to, she was making sure that I would keep my word. Maybe I didn't understand the language, but I knew that she was counting on me. Not everything had to be said with words.

I lost sight of her as I endured another breakfast of fruits, olives, and smoked fish. It wasn't until we were properly dressed and escorted to the front of the villa that I noticed her conversing with someone that I presumed was her mother. I watched as the elegantly attired older woman was carried off in the first litter but not before saying something that made the girl anxious and edgy. Seconds later, a house slave beckoned for me to get into a litter with three other girls.

The sun hadn't yet reached its peak so I figured the event must start at noon. If Ryn were here, he'd make some comment like, "Bull gorging at high noon!" *Well, you're not here, Ryn. This is one mess I've got to deal with myself.* I couldn't let Wendell get himself killed. Looking back at the girl who was now stepping into her litter, something dawned on me. *She was looking for someone!* How could I have been so unaware as to not notice her hand gestures last night?

All I had to do was make sure I was seated next to her and pretend that I had spotted whoever it was. I'd point in Wendell's direction once he appeared in the arena. She was bound to create a scene and I would use the diversion to get that stupid kid out. As our litter got closer and closer to the arena, I felt my pulse quicken. I finally had a plan.

It was controlled pandemonium in front of the arena when we arrived. The entire city of Thera was waiting to get inside. Gates seemed to open at once and a flood of people raced in so quickly that the air filled with dust. Our entourage was taken to a main gate that led to a stairwell and corridor that I was all too familiar with. We were given the most exclusive seats in the arena, overlooking the center of the ring. I stalled, pretending to drop something, so that I could sit next to the girl once she arrived.

Across from us were the city's officials and royal members. Even though the expanse of the arena separated us, I could see by their attire that they were not ordinary citizens and neither were we. If this was an *Imagine Dragons* concert I'd be ecstatic. As it was, I was grateful to have the commanding view I needed to keep my eye on Wendell.

I'd never seen a crowd as wild and frenetic as this one. Not even our Super Bowls could come close to the unbridled energy I felt. It was palpable and I was getting drawn in. Suddenly, a clang of cymbals rang out and all movement stopped. There had to be at least fifty cymbal players simultaneously signaling the start of the event.

A tall, heavily adorned man, flanked by two guards, walked to the center of the arena and spoke. Five or six words at most. Then, more cymbals followed by a procession of men and boys waving red, yellow and gold banners in the air. The cheering was deafening. I held my breath and watched as the procession circled the arena.

Wendell had to be part of it but it was impossible for me to recognize him.

So much for my plan. If there was any chance of getting him out before the bull jumping or whatever-it-was they were going to do, it was too late. The boys disappeared behind the corrals and, one-by-one, the bulls were led out into the arena. Wild, black bulls that snorted and kicked their hooves. Four bulls in all. One for each corner. The crowd went wild.

I held my breath as teams of three surrounded each bull. One boy stood in front, one in the rear and one off to the side. I tried to zero in on each section, hoping to spot Wendell. I didn't. Maybe he wasn't in the first set.

The action moved like a carefully choreographed dance. The boy in front waited for the bull to lower its head and then ran towards it, grabbing the horns in a handstand leap over the top of the animal's head. I couldn't tell if it was the bull that lifted the boy or if it was shear strength and agility but I knew one thing. Wendell was doomed.

Chapter Forty-five:

Wendell

Holy crap! We got to walk about a block and a half when out of nowhere this giant crowd of crazies appeared. Screaming! Yelling! Waving their arms at us! Was this kind of stuff what made Justin Bieber so nuts? I didn't blame him. The crowd got bigger and bigger as it followed us up to the arena.

By the time we reached our gate, I would have sold my iPad for a pair of earplugs. The guards moved us quickly into a special area reserved for Those Who Are Going to Get Gored to Death. We sat on hard benches behind a line-up of corrals. The bulls smelled worse than ever and were really twitchy. The flies hovering around their eyes and butts didn't help. I watched as the bulls switched their tails and stomped the ground. The only good news was that these were the smaller bulls. The black ones. The ones that Yidini and Sima thought would be fun to jump over. I wondered about Yidini and Sima. They'd probably think jumping off Mt. Rushmore would be fun, too.

Not only did the bulls stink, but they blocked my view of the audience. I could see part of the upper tiers but not everything. Crap. That meant Aeden, wherever she was, wouldn't be able to find me either. Not until I got into the ring.

Slaves walked back and forth in front of us, offering us water and diluted wine. Heck, even prisoners are given a better last meal. It was impossible to figure out what was going on. People were screaming and shouting so loud that if one of their volcanoes erupted, they'd never know it until the hot stuff started flying.

Next thing I knew, cymbals clanged and everyone shut up. Everyone! It was like someone turned on the mute button to the TV. From my scenic view of bulls' rear ends, it was hard to get a good look at what was happening in the ring. I stood up for a split second. Two men were walking someone really important into the center of the arena. The guy said something and the cymbals started clanging again.

Someone elbowed me to stand up and follow the line. Like I had a choice. We paraded around the ring waving our banners as people screamed and yelled. I wanted to scream and yell, too. *Get me the heck out of here!*

It was a relief to sit back down behind the stinking bulls even though I knew it would only be for a few minutes. We put our banners on the ground in front of us and waited. Four bulls were led to the different corners of the arena. Then, groups of three marched over to their assigned playmate. I took a deep breath and started counting the line where I was sitting. One-two-three, one-two-three, one-two-three, one-two-three . . . I wasn't in the first line-up. Maybe if I got lucky, it would take them the entire afternoon and I'd be home free for another day.

So much for fantasy mind games. I knew better. I leaned in and watched to see what the contenders were doing, hoping I could imitate their moves without getting myself killed. *Where the heck are you, Aeden? Thought you were going to have a plan.*

The bull threw me into the air the last time but that wasn't what was supposed to happen. I was supposed to run dead-on towards the thing, grab its horns and hoist myself. If that were the case, Ringling Brothers would have found a way to offer me a contract on the spot.

My stomach started to churn as I tried to keep its contents from spewing all over the place. The first match happened so quickly that before I knew it, those guys all returned to their seats and I was number one in the next group going into the arena. Number one. The bull runner. On a suicide mission for sure.

Chapter Forty-six:

Kitane

The girl who did my make-up found a way to sit next to me even though she was not in my litter. Together we could peruse the crowd and look for the demon girl. Most likely that evil spirit would return to the same place tomorrow. If all went as planned, I would bring her the little surprise that Ariadnh was procuring for me in the marketplace.

The Taurokathapsia began in the usual way with cymbals, a procession and the announcement from the city leader. The first round of bull jumping was non-eventful. No one was gorged, no one fell and no one was trampled. The acrobatics were mediocre. I watched as the contenders hoisted themselves over the bulls' heads and somersaulted down.

Maybe she never witnessed a Taurokathapsia before, because the girl next to me was at the edge of her seat. Leaning forward, she held her breath as she watched the jumping. Occasionally her eyes darted from side to side and that's when I realized she was probably searching for the demon girl and not fixating on the boys.

The sun was at its peak and surely hair as bright as flames would stand out in the crowd. I didn't expect the demon girl to be seated anywhere above us because those areas were reserved for the wealthiest of families, like mine. Below us were the guards and centurions so she couldn't possibly be there. I whispered to the girl next to me that we needed to focus on each and every seat across and around us before the afternoon shadows took over. She nodded and continued to stare straight ahead.

By now the second group of contenders had started to approach the bulls. I couldn't help it. I opened my mouth to yawn just as my eyes started to close. That's when the girl poked me and pointed straight past the ring to the center section. By the time I focused, it was too late. Everyone in that section was standing and screaming, waving their arms. They must have blocked the demon girl from view.

Whatever happened in the ring had only taken a second and I missed it. Worse yet, the demon girl was no longer visible.

Chapter Forty-seven:

Aeden

Everything was over before it even started. It was awful. No way to help Wendell. I kept my eyes glued to the arena in order to spot him. It wasn't easy. All of the boys were dressed alike and their hair was styled the same way. Only one thing set that little jerk apart—the way he swaggered about like he was some hotshot. The bad news was that he wasn't about to swagger in front of those bulls. No bravado today. I had to look for a kid who was out of his league.

Like dabbing numbers on a BINGO card, I eliminated two quads immediately. The ones in front of us. Wendell wasn't in those sections. That left the two rear sections. I watched for anything that appeared out of the ordinary and that's when I saw it. One of the kids was looking up at the crowd. No one does that. Same deal as being in a play, they should be focused on the stage, not the audience. I knew immediately it was Wendell.

Acting quickly, I jabbed my elbow into the arm of the girl sitting next to me, hoping she would start some sort of commotion. I wasn't particular. Any kind of diversion would have done nicely.

I turned to face her, hoping to see what she would do. In that split second, I witnessed something so astonishing, so bizarre and so unlikely that I was stunned. The crowd went berserk and everyone screamed at once. People waving, cheering, shrieking.

Wendell had managed not only to leap over that bull but to jump so high that he did a complete tumblesault in the air before landing straight up on the bull's back. The blood raced to my face as I watched the boy, who was positioned at the rear of the bull, hold out his hand and lead Wendell off of the beast.

It was insanity. Like the whole arena got struck by lightning. That's how wild and terrifying everything seemed. It was at least a full half hour before the events could continue. By then, it was too late to do anything that would get Wendell out of there.

Chapter Forty-eight:

Wendell

Aunt Eleanor recites some stupid mantra every morning when she wakes up. I know because I can hear her mutter something like, "You are deserving, you are gifted, you are whatever . . ." I added a mantra of my own when I walked into the arena and straight towards that bull.

One with the universe. Nothing matters. One with the universe. Nothing matters. One with the . . .

I was standing so close that I could smell his reeking breath when the worst pain ever tore into my *cajones* and I jumped into the air. The pin! The pin that I used to secure the flap on my loincloth had come loose and jabbed me. The shocking jolt to my privates sent me into the air without any help from anyone. I had no choice but to grab onto the bull's horns since they were coming right at me.

Twisting my body in an attempt to alleviate the pain in my groin resulted in my bending over into a ball. By that time I was well over the stupid bull's head with my own head tucked towards my knees. It was over before I knew it.

I was in mid-air performing a stunt that only the Flying Wallendas could dream about. I felt my feet land on the bull's back as I stood at attention hoping to dislodge the pin. At that point, I didn't care who saw *what.*

Latching onto an arm that was stretched out towards me, I squeezed it and jumped off of the thing. The pin must have fallen out because I was no longer writhing in pain. I was, however, dazed and dizzy.

As I staggered back to the area behind the corral, I heard the crowd explode with noise. So much for Aeden figuring out a way to get me out of this nightmare. Harry Houdini couldn't even do that. I was on my own and I had to think fast.

Chapter Forty-nine:

Kitane

I could see Ariadnh pushing her way towards us as the crowd continued to explode. I stood up and motioned for her to stay where she was, near the balcony railing. Then, I grabbed the arm of the girl sitting next to me and we both made our way to the edge of our section where Ariadnh was standing. From there, all three of us hurried into the corridor by the stairwell.

No one bothered to notice. They were all cheering and waving. Before I could say a word, Ariadnh spoke.

"I will have it for you tonight, mistress. The arrangements were made. Finding a tiny one with a sharp sting was not easy. I must return at dusk to get it."

"Good," I said. "Bring it directly to my room and put it inside the small clay vessel with the lid. When we attend the Taurokathapsia tomorrow, I shall have you place the linen sack over the vessel and empty the contents of that vessel directly into the sack. You must be exceedingly careful."

I could see the fear on Ariadnh's face. The girl standing beside me could see it as well.

"It won't be able to bite you once the linen is secured. It is such a small thing that I myself will be able to conceal it in my clothing when we attend tomorrow's events."

"Are you planning to kill the *gift*, mistress?"

"The *gift*?"

"Yes, did you not see the miraculous way in which he rose into the air above the bull? Only a special gift from the gods would have that kind of power."

So that's why the audience is stirring with excitement. I can't believe I missed it. While I was so intent on finding the one who released the special sacrifice, I missed the 'gift' himself doing his sorcery. This changes everything. Ariadnh has given me an idea and I will act upon it tomorrow.

"That is enough for now, Ariadnh. You may join the other slaves."

As she nodded and walked off, I whispered to the girl.

"If we can stop the *gift*, then neither of us will be forced into marriage."

"Nai," she replied.

"Tomorrow is the day of the white bulls," I continued. "When they send our special boy into the arena, we will make sure he is not alone."

We returned to our seats in time to watch mediocre bull jumping and a final procession of the contenders.

"Do you know which one is the *gift?*" I asked the girl, expecting nothing more than a *yes* or *no*. She answered without hesitation, and in that instant, I knew I could trust her.

It was now up to Ariadnh. She had to procure that newly born viper if we had any chance of changing our fates.

Chapter Fifty:

Aeden

That girl was up to something, I knew it. I also knew that whatever it *was*, it wasn't going to happen today. Tomorrow, perhaps? I couldn't be sure. It would be another twenty-four hours before the next opportunity came. It wasn't looking good. I doubted very much that Wendell could pull off another stunt like the one he did earlier in the arena.

As I sank down on my cot and stared at the night sky through the small window in my room, I realized that there was only one thing that could save him—my acting skills. I had it all planned. I would do the one thing that would get anyone arrested in a theater. Yell "FIRE!" Only, I wouldn't be yelling the word, I would be creating the illusion.

At high noon, with pieces of small reflective metals and stones that I found on the beach and crushed into my hair like glitter, I would approach the corrals from behind the winding corridor and then race into the arena the minute it was Wendell's turn to do whatever stunt they had planned for him.

I'd scream at the top of my lungs, wave my arms and act as if I was having a tantrum. It wouldn't be too hard. Growing up, I had plenty of exposure to that kind of behavior whenever my brother Ryn didn't get his way. The audience and the guards would be so preoccupied with me that Wendell could make a run for it and I would follow. I just had to be sure that he knew where to meet me. Amid my yelling and screaming, I'd shout for him to meet me at the harbor.

We could always sneak onto a boat or hide under the docks. Maybe it wasn't the most detailed, well thought out plan, but it was better than sitting and waiting for the kid to get gored.

Dozing on and off was the only luxury I was going to allow myself that night. I had to sneak out before dawn, get to the beach, hunt around for the reflective stuff and get back in time to prepare for the second festival day. I would be exhausted before I ever started.

Chapter Fifty-one:

Wendell

It wasn't enough that I was nearly killed on top of that bull, but I had to march around the arena again waving that stupid banner as the cymbals clanged in my ears. I gave up trying to find Aeden. She was probably having a blast watching this spectacle. Heck, for all I know maybe they were even serving her some kind of Ancient Greek cotton candy.

We exited out the main gates before the crowd did. Then we had to hoof it back to our villa where I collapsed once again on my cot. Yidini and Sima managed to do okay on their bulls. "Okay" meaning they still were in possession of their extremities and other valued body parts.

The slaves brought us bread with tomato paste and watery wine. For dessert, dried fruit. We were once again washed, toweled dry and anointed with smelly oil. Might as well have been a sardine in a cannery.

Today's episode was torture, with or without the pin in my privates. I imagined tomorrow would be worse but was too scared to ask. As it turned out, Yidini couldn't help but tell me.

"You amazed them today, Widina. That means they will bring you the biggest and most magnificent white bull tomorrow. It is something Sima and I can only dream about."

I'm dreaming, too. Only it's called a nightmare. I gulped and asked the question I was dreading.

"Other than the color, what's the difference between the white bull and the one I had to jump over today?"

Sima's eyes lit up. He couldn't wait to share the bad news.

"The white bull is much larger and unruly. It bucks and kicks. That's not so bad."

"Not so bad?" I was almost screaming.

"No, it is only bad when the bull decides to charge at the jumper. There is no stopping it. The jumper must be ready to get out of its way or use the opportunity to grab the horns and make the leap. If the jumper merely gets out of the way, he is immediately disqualified."

Then Yidini had to put his two cents in.

"By disqualified, Sima means shamed, disgraced, dishonored---"

"I get the idea."

Talk about playing the odds. If I got disgraced, what was the worst thing that would happen? They'd escort me out of there? I figured that was much better than the grand prize of having to fight to the death and then be stuck in some arranged marriage. I made a mental note to get the hell away from the white bull if he decided to charge at me. The way I looked at it, it was 50-50. The bull would either charge at me or stand there and grunt. Either way, I wasn't looking forward to the next day.

Suddenly, I realized something. I had another option. What if I deliberately got the bull to chase me around the arena until I was at one of the corral gates? I could jump that sucker in a second and bolt for the nearest exit. Aeden was bound to see me. I'd make sure of it.

That night, I fell asleep mumbling one sentence over and over again. *A bullfighter never thinks about his own death.* It was on a poster I had seen at our school's foreign language fair. The matador was waving a red cape and the bull's head was down. Lucky for him. The bull wasn't one of the white ones.

I woke up to the familiar smell of dead fish. Well, dried, dead fish to be exact. They had a stench I could recognize from a hundred feet. The slaves also left a platter of fruit and some juice. Nothing had been touched yet. Yidini and

Sima were still sleeping. Guess none of us heard the friendly wake-up call from the guards.

My eyes felt gritty and sandy as I rubbed them with my thumb and index finger. I was in no rush to hear the schedule they had in store for me today so I came up with my own.

Period 1—Deep cleansing because the bull only wants to gore clean victims.

Period 2—Processional march so that the victim will be worn out before he gets to the arena.

Period 3—Arrive at the ring for more marching, just to be sure.

Period 4—Sit and sweat it out waiting for your turn.

Period 5—Death sentence.

Pretty much, I nailed that one, with two exceptions: no black bulls in sight and a zillion flies swarming over the white ones. Maybe it was because the white bulls stunk more. I don't know. The only thing I was aware of was the fact that the white bulls were *really* pissed.

Occasionally, one of the big horseflies would venture out of the corral and buzz us as we sat on the benches waiting to be called up into the arena. It was impossible to hear myself think with all the noise and screaming from the bloodthirsty fans. Not so much of a *Go Team* than a *Go Get Killed*.

This time there were three larger rings in front, each with its own Behemoth. Two of the bulls had some small brown spots on them, but the other was solid white. Solid white and at least seventy-five pounds heavier. I didn't need a clairvoyant for this one. I already knew. The biggest, nastiest, foul breath animal was going to be mine. When no one was looking, I ripped the red banner that I had carried into the processional off of its wooden pole, balled it up, and shoved it into my loincloth. I figured if I couldn't divert that beast, at least I could protect my progeny.

Chapter Fifty-two:

Aeden

I gave up on falling asleep, knowing that if I did, I might miss my only opportunity to sneak down to the beach. Instead, I stared into the semi-darkness, letting out long, deep breaths as my shoulders sank deeper into my bed. I must have stayed in that position for at least a few hours, turning only when it was necessary. Wide awake, it was easy to hear the footsteps in the corridor. There were no other sounds to mask them.

My body tightened as I forced myself to remain still. The footsteps were getting closer. Probably the guards making their rounds. I held still. Not the guards. They would walk briskly. Soles pounding into the tile. This was different. The footsteps were lighter, tentative, pausing every few feet.

Slowly, I positioned myself on my side so that I could stare at the archway to my room. By now, the footsteps were only a few yards away. At least

I was awake. I could scream if I had to. Holding still, I kept my eyes fixed on the entryway. That's when I heard the voice. It was the girl from the arena.

I stood up quickly, wrapping the linen blanket around me as she approached. Her voice was barely audible and I struggled to make sense of what she was saying. No use. The words were garble to me.

Next thing I knew, she grabbed me by the wrist, motioned for me to be silent (as if talking to her was really a possibility) and led me out of my room and into the corridor. My sandals barely made a sound as I followed her to her room.

With a few oil lamps lit and some sconces on the walls, I could see another girl sitting on one of the floor cushions. As I stepped in closer, I recognized her. It was the slave girl. Ariana? Arianda? I had only heard her name mentioned once.

The girl from the arena picked up one of the oil lamps and carried it to the corner of the room where a small rounded clay jar stood against the wall. Unlike most of the jars I had seen, this one had a lid.

Holding the lamp over the jar, the girl spoke. At times her words were directed at me. Otherwise, to her slave. All I could do was nod and shake my head. Then, the slave girl held up a small sack with a tie ribbon. Quickly, she knelt down by the jar and in one motion, removed the lid and placed the sack directly over it.

I thought my heart would stop right then and there. My brother, during his grade school years, was an expert on that kind of thing.

Shhh, Aeden. It'll be lots of fun. We dump the box upside down into the pillowcase and then we can let the mouse out in the kitchen when mom's not looking.

It was mice. It was bugs. It was even a nasty horned toad. But somehow, I knew that this was no innocent trick. Whatever the slave girl was about to put into the linen sack was far more dangerous than any childhood prank my brother could come up with.

I took a small step back, not daring to take my eyes off of the slave girl or the one from the arena. In an instant, the slave girl dumped the contents into the sack and fastened it with the ribbon before handing it to the girl from the arena.

At first I thought the oil lamps were burning brighter because I could make out what was wriggling in that sack. A snake! It had to be a snake. Nothing moves like that. The girl from the arena then placed the sack back into the jar before turning to face me. She whispered a few words and then put her index finger to her lips.

I nodded and did the same as I walked backwards towards the archway to the corridor.

Three things became frighteningly clear: the girl was about to do something horrific with the snake; I had inadvertently become a part of her plan; and worst of all, it wasn't the oil lamps that were getting stronger. It was the sky breaking through the horizon. I had missed my opportunity to get to the beach.

Chapter Fifty-three:

Kitane

The girl was as pleased as I was that Ariadnh had secured the viper. It was small but effective. One bite and its victim would not be able to see the sun for days. Ariadnh would carry the small sack to the arena this afternoon and hand it to me once we were seated.

The processional would merit thunderous applause. No one would be able to keep still after yesterday's performance. With the spectators waving and yelling, the girl and I would slip out of our section, through the corridor and down to the corrals. Once the *gift* started to make his way towards the white bull, I would open the sack and toss the viper at his feet. It would be easy to pick out which contender was the *gift*. He would be given the largest, most contentious and unpredictable of all the bulls. Any normal contender would face his death for certain but not this one. He had a demon girl to protect him.

Still . . . I had the viper. No sorcery would be able to stop its venom. My only obstacle was getting to the *gift* before he reached the inside ring with the white bull.

Luckily, the girl I entrusted had agreed to use her charms with the guards so that they would be distracted while I made my way to the corrals. When Ariadnh and the girl had left my room, I walked over to the jar, bent down and spoke.

Do not betray us, little viper. You are working against some powerful sorcery.

Chapter Fifty-four:

Wendell

If that was Aeden's plan, I didn't know *whose* side she was on—me or the bull. Directly in front of me stood a bull the size of a reconnaissance vehicle, snorting and pounding its hooves into the sand. There were two other rings on either side but those bulls looked as if they belonged in a petting zoo compared to mine.

At once, I was directed to stand up and approach my bull as two other guys marched towards theirs. I felt like yelling, "Trade Ya!" but it would have been a waste of breath. I was maybe eight or nine feet from what I now refer to as *the white death* when all hell broke loose. And by all hell, that's putting it mildly.

The crowd was screaming and bellowing, same as yesterday, only they were already out of their seats. I took a step forward and reached into my loincloth to grab the red banner but I never got a chance.

"Watch out, Wen-DELL! She's going to throw a snake at you! A snake at you! Poisonous! Watch out, Dell! S–N–A–K–E! Snake!"

I looked away from the bull long enough to see that same nutcase girl from the other day racing out of the corral. Behind her, Aeden was screaming her lungs out. It took my mind a second to register that it was Aeden. Her hair was done up in what I could best describe as my Aunt Eleanor on her way to a Bar Mitzvah. It was Aeden all right. Screaming about a snake. As if I didn't have enough crap going on. *Is that how you plan to help me? By scaring the hell out of me?*

Aeden's screams got louder and she started to wave her arms. *Sure, that's going to scare a snake.* By now the guards were after her and I lost track of where the nutcase girl was because more guards were running into the arena.

Next thing I knew the bull let out a huge snort, bent his head down, and came right at me. So did something else. *The snake maybe?* Whatever it was, it barely grazed my face as it landed in front of the bull. That white beast bent forward, kicked up its rear legs and then bent its colossal head way, *way* down. A voice screamed in my head. *This is your mega moment, Dell T. No time to run. Grab that sucker by the horns!*

So I did. I latched onto those horns, the adrenaline pumping through my veins like crazy. The bull thrust its head up giving me the momentum I needed to fling myself over its body. My head was tucked down so far below my knees that I swore I could have looked up my own butt. I rolled off that thing in a somersault, landing upright on the ground. This time there was no "spotter" to help me. I had seconds before that bull would realize I was still in the arena with him.

Disgraced or not, I had to get out of there. I whipped the red banner from my loincloth and held it in front of me as I tried to back away. That was the instant when I saw it —small, black, coiled up and ready to strike at my ankle. If that wasn't enough to scare me senseless, the stupid bull turned around and was glaring right at me.

Frantic, I tossed the red banner over the snake and made a run for it. Yep, the run of shame, disgrace and ultimate demise. Only that didn't happen. People started cheering. Really, really loud. By the time I had made it back to the corral seating area, the audience was going nuts.

What I didn't see, because I was too busy trying to save my own hide, was the bull stomping over the red banner until he managed to crush the snake. Next thing I knew, two of the bigger guards rushed over to me, one on each side, and held my arms straight up in the air. They were either going to tear my limbs off, or parade me around like a hero.

Please let it be the hero thing. Please let it be the hero thing.

They spun me around so that I faced at least three quarters of the arena. Cymbals started clanging and people were waving their arms in the air. I should've enjoyed the moment. Instead, my knees started to feel weak and salty saliva filled my mouth.

Don't ruin it, Dell T, by puking in front of everyone.

I swallowed hard and waited until the nausea passed, using those few seconds to try and spot Aeden. It was impossible. Every time I saw someone who might have been her, it turned out they weren't.

I did see the nutcase girl. She was standing near one of the columns by the corral and crying. Unbelievable. I figured she was crying because I was still alive. Talk about bloodthirsty. *What did I ever do to you, girl?* I mean, why would someone lose it just because a guy didn't get gored to death today? Unless . . . she had money or whatever they use, riding on this event. No wonder she threw a snake at me. She was rooting for the four legged team.

Well, tough going girl. Looks like Dell T won today!

Then, I realized something. Today's win meant tomorrow's fight to the death. Suddenly, I wasn't so thrilled about my new-found status.

Chapter Fifty-five:

Kitane

Everything had gone wrong. Everything. I don't know how long I stood by the columns near the corral sobbing my eyes out. It was only when Ariadnh approached me with a dry cloth for my tears that I realized I needed to get back to my seat. The girl who had tried to help me was a few feet away staring at the *gift* as they paraded him about.

I couldn't blame her at all for what had happened. She did a spectacular job of diverting the guards with the gibberish she screamed at the *gift* as he walked towards the bull. I thought perhaps she would beguile one of the guards but she was smarter than that. She knew that she had to get all of their attention. What better way than to create a shrieking scene.

It was my aim that was off. Not close enough for the viper to strike. Now, the thing lay dead in the arena, crushed by the white bull, like any hope I might have had to escape my awful fate.

"You still have one day left," Ariadnh whispered. "You'll think of something, mistress."

"We must return to our seats, Ariadnh. Go get the girl and tell her to hurry along with us."

A few minutes later, the three of us stared blankly at the day's concluding ceremony. I could tell that the girl was visibly shaken and upset. Leaning over, I touched her arm and told her that we would find another way to stop the *gift* tomorrow.

I didn't think the day could get any worse but I was wrong. No sooner did we return to the villa when Mother summoned for me to meet her in the small atrium near her room. *Had she realized that I had been away from my seat? Did she know it was me in the arena with the viper? Impossible. She could not have seen me that closely.* I tried to maintain my composure as I sat next to her on the stone bench.

"I have summoned you to let you know that you will be betrothed following the conclusion of the Taurokathapsia tomorrow. It has been decided."

Before I could utter a word, my mother continued to speak, punctuating every word as if they were pins meant to prick me.

"Your father realized, beyond a doubt, that the sacrificial gift meant for the gods, was one of the contenders. No ordinary boy could dance over the bulls as if they were toads."

I took a breath and spoke.

"So he is to be my suitor?"

"Spit on the ground at once for uttering such a thought!"

I did as she said and waited for her response.

"The *gift* must be offered to the gods if we are to survive. Tomorrow, at noon, is the fight-to-the death in the arena. If the opponent defeats the *gift,* then you are to be betrothed to *that* contender and the *gift's* body will become a burnt offering upon the altar. Your father has already made the arrangements with the leaders of Thera."

"And if it is the *gift* that defeats his adversary?"

"Then the gods will smile on Thera and Akrotiri. The *gift* will be taken immediately for a grand sacrifice upon the knoll that overlooks the harbor and another suitor will be chosen for you."

Words could not form in my mouth.

"Don't stand there staring at the ground, Kitane. This is as it should be. And do not think that the demon girl will be able to rescue the *gift* this time. Surely, the guards will seize her if she makes a move."

"No one has seen that demon girl, Mother."

"All the better. Now go enjoy the company of the other girls. Tomorrow you will be spoken for."

She stood up and motioned for her slave, who was standing at the other side of the atrium, to approach. I muttered something and hurried back to my room, trying not to burst out in tears. My only hope was that Ariadnh's words would hold true.

"You'll think of something, mistress."

Chapter Fifty-six:

Aeden

My God! Was she trying to kill the bull or Wendell? It was impossible to tell. She was crying her eyes out when it was all over with and had to be escorted back to her seat by her slave. I had to admit, Wendell acted quickly and intelligently for once in his life. He threw that banner on the snake and made a good run for it. Too bad he couldn't get past the corrals. Time was running out for both of us and I had to come up with something by tomorrow. *You told yourself that two days ago, Aeden. What's taking you so long?*

The girl sniffled and sobbed intermittently during the remainder of the program, pausing occasionally to tap my arm and mutter a few words. Once we got back to our villa, she and her slave went back to their room and I wandered about in the courtyards and atriums like someone who was dazed after hearing bad news. The stairwell to the rooftop garden where we watched the nighttime procession was no longer blocked by its usual centurions. I thought perhaps I might be able to get a good view of Wendell's villa and any possible unguarded entrances where I could slip in. There were a few daylight hours left and I had to act quickly.

I gasped when I took in the expanse of the city. In broad daylight, with no one blocking the view, I could see every nuance of the place from its winding streets to its huge marketplace, harbor and beaches. I could even make out boats in the distance. I should have been acutely aware of it before, but I wasn't. That harbor beacon seemed to emit some sort of energy. Its light flickered and danced with a pulse that seemed to energize the harbor. Then again, all of that could have been my imagination. I was overwrought and feeling helpless about the situation Wendell had gotten himself into.

Pull yourself together Aeden. You're feeling vulnerable and you're letting your imagination go wild. FOCUS!

I fixed my attention to Wendell's villa and studied it carefully. The main gates were guarded as were the gates on all four sides. However, as I watched the movement in and about the place, I could see that there was some sort of doorway on the far right hand corner, probably a good fifteen or twenty feet from one of the gates. If I could manage to get in unseen and stay that way, I had a decent chance of finding him. We could both get out that door and make a dash towards the beach.

With no time to waste, I raced down the stairs and through the first courtyard. My heart was starting to pound as I headed to the balcony where I had slipped out once before. This time I knew Wendell would be in the villa. My palms and knees hadn't had a chance to heal from my last attempt at this and I dreaded the thought of getting even more cut up on the rock and brush.

The balcony was directly across from a smaller courtyard. I made a dash for it when someone rounded the corner from the other direction and smashed directly into me, our heads bumping with the right amount of force to take the breath out of both of us. It was the girl from the arena. The crying girl. The one with the snake. Her slave was a few feet behind and rushed over to make sure we were all right.

Tears started to form in the corner of my eyes and I let out a small sniffle. Not so much from pain as frustration. I couldn't very well go jumping down from a balcony right in front of them.

The girl immediately took my hand and said something. I imagine it was an apology of sorts and I nodded. I could see from the way the black kohl stained her eyes that she was still distraught.

Well, that makes two of us. Now what?

She continued to talk when all of sudden her slave shrieked and pointed to a small black spider on the wall behind us. I'd never seen anything like it —red blotchy markings on its abdomen and long, black legs. I took a few steps back and held still, expecting the girl and her slave to walk away.

The look on the girl's face changed from misery to ecstasy in a matter of seconds. She waved an arm, said something to the slave and watched as the poor girl ran off only to return in a matter of minutes with a small lidded vessel.

In the meantime, I listened intently as the girl spilled out what I believed to be some new plan that would ultimately kill Wendell, one way or the other. I was certain of it. There would be no bulls in the arena tomorrow, only the fighters. I had gotten my answer after all. It wasn't the bull she wanted dead.

Chapter Fifty-seven:

Wendell

I was one step away from a complete and total meltdown. Yidini and Sima didn't notice. They were too busy stuffing themselves with bits of roasted meat on skewers and popping olives into their mouths like popcorn. It was after dark and we were back in our room having survived day two of the bull ceremony.

"I have never known anyone as fortunate as you, Widina, to ride the back of the white bull in one motion," Yidini said as he popped another olive into his mouth. "Why aren't you eating anything?"

Because I'm scared out of my gourd that I'll be dead tomorrow and that kind of makes you lose your appetite.

"I'm not very hungry. So, can you tell me what will happen at tomorrow's fight?"

"It is a shame you have never seen this event before. Tomorrow is the most spectacular of all.

Acrobats and dancers will perform in the arena. Then, the two contenders walk the outer circle as the patrons reach out to touch them. Once they have walked completely around the arena, they will stand on a high platform in the middle of the ring and fight to the death."

I tried to stay focused.

"Who's the other contender?"

"Why it is one of the boys who jumped the other white bull while you leapt over yours."

I didn't recall anyone jumping over anything, but then again, I was too busy looking out for my own hide, that someone could have launched a rocket-propelled grenade and I wouldn't have noticed.

Yidini kept talking.

"There were two other bulls and two jumpers. Both of them succeeded but one of them was slow and clumsy. He lost the honor of fighting with you. The other was that tall, muscular boy from Crete. We saw him the first day we were brought to this villa. Sima had never seen anyone with so much strength in his arms."

Good. Maybe Sima would like to take a crack at that guy.

The more Yidini told me, the more I started to freak-out. I tried to envision all sorts of scenarios that would get me out of tomorrow's ordeal, like the guy choking to death on an olive or getting bitten by a scorpion.

A few minutes later the slaves came in to wash our feet and replace the watery wine with more watery wine. I guzzled it down hoping it would render me senseless. It didn't. All it did was make me want to pee.

I spent the rest of the night walking in and out of the commode until I finally fell asleep. I don't know what I was dreaming about, but when the guard pounded on the archway the next morning I was so groggy that I sat up and pounded a fist straight into the wall. A fist with my right hand. My good hand.

Nice going, Dell T. You just threw the fight.

Chapter Fifty-eight:

Kitane

"This is our only chance, Ariadnh," I said as we walked back to my room. "The spider you have captured is deadly. We must make sure that it bites *both* contenders. It will paralyze them and pull them into such a deep delirium that it will be days until they regain consciousness. *If* they regain consciousness. Father will know that the gods have been angered and will not force a betrothal upon me. I will have been spared."

"And what of the other girl, mistress?"

"She will be spared as well. No royal family will dare to anger the gods. I explained this carefully to the girl and she will do her part to ensure that we do not fail this time."

"How so, mistress?"

"At the start of the ceremony, both contenders walk the circle around the ring. Instead of watching them from our seats above the general crowd, we will join the other patrons to reach out and acknowledge the fighters. When both of them are close enough together, I shall have you release the spider onto one of their arms while the girl and I keep them otherwise occupied. The spider will undoubtedly bite and jump, for that is what they do. When it does, it will land on the other contender and bite him as well. Then, we wait."

"Are you certain this will work, mistress? I do not wish to be bitten."

"Remove the vessel's lid, tip the vessel forward and give it a quick thrust towards the first fighter. Be sure to step back."

"I understand, mistress."

"Good. Now secure the vessel and do not say a word to anyone. Quick! Before we are seen."

Ariadnh did not waste a second. I watched as she disappeared down the corridor. By this time tomorrow, I expected to be free from any and all marital arrangements.

Chapter Fifty-nine:

Aeden

Either that girl had an ironclad reason to kill Wendell, or she was completely insane. Her emotions ran hot and cold depending upon whatever scheme she came up with to murder him. Worst of all, she thought I was her accomplice. She smiled at me as she and her slave walked down the corridor to the guest rooms. I stood for a moment, trying to regain my composure when a group of giggling girls appeared out of nowhere and walked towards the balcony, ruining any chance I had of getting over the wall to Wendell's villa.

I turned and walked inside the main courtyard hoping that the gigglers would disappear in a few minutes so that I could get on with my plan. Even in daylight, the frescos on the walls were as unsettling as they were when I first saw them. Volcanic eruptions, dolphins jumping wildly, bulls tossing bloody riders and finally that girl staring at the man in the bloody loincloth as the women around her danced.

My eyes darted from scene to scene. With the exception of a volcanic explosion, I had pretty much experienced all that this island offered. Well, maybe not all . . . the girl approaching the man in the bloody loincloth . . . the women dancing . . . *OH MY GOD! OH MY GOD! How could I have been so dense! It was a betrothal! OH MY GOD! The man who won the fight got betrothed and married! OH MY GOD! That girl is the one who will be forced to marry the victor! That's why she wants to kill Wendell. She knows he's favored to win!*

This wasn't about her wanting to kill Wendell; it was about her *not* wanting to get married. How could I have missed it? No wonder she tried to throw a snake at him. It all made sense. Now she's armed with a poisonous spider and will no doubt find a way to have it bite that kid. I ran back to the balcony hoping the girls had left but instead, they were joined by six or seven more. All of them were talking and laughing, and from the looks of it, they weren't about to leave any time soon.

Calm down, Aeden. If you can't get to Wendell, at least you can try to get to that spider and kill it first.

I hurried toward the direction where the girl and her slave were headed, figuring that they were going to stash that spider in their room. Luckily, no one saw me. I managed to creep down the corridor until I found the right quarters where they were residing. I rapped on their archway praying that they were not inside. My breath came in small spurts and my hands were all sweaty and clammy.

No answer. I pounded the doorway again before finally working up the courage to step inside. There was still some sunlight coming through the small windows, enough to illuminate the room. My sandals made a soft tap on the stone floor as I moved further inside. First, to the shelves where the clothing was stored. Nothing. Then to the corners of the room. Nothing. To the commode. To the bedding. Under the cots. Nothing. Nothing. Nothing.

That slave girl had to have taken the spider to another location in the villa. It would be like searching the Hermitage in St. Petersburg. Futile. I could feel a slight tremor in my hands as I turned to face the corridor. My body reacted in its own way to my fear. Suddenly, I heard footsteps and froze. Was the girl returning with her slave? I couldn't very well be seen stepping out of their room.

Time to practice your acting skills, Aeden.

Immediately, I sat down on one of the cots and began to sob. I know. I know. My brother always said it was a low down girly thing to do in order to get what I wanted. Low down or not, it wasn't as if I was bursting with options. I held still and waited for them to enter.

The full pose was in place. Hands wringing. Sobs and sniffles. All I needed was for the other "actors" to walk on set. I was ready to be comforted by the girl who thought I was her ally. So when a house slave took a step into the room, I gasped.

The middle aged woman said something, bent her head down, and quickly rushed to light the oil lamps and the sconces. Seconds later, I left the room and made my way to my own quarters. It was useless. I couldn't help Wendell escape and I couldn't find that damn spider. Not tonight anyway.

I had one more chance—in a packed arena with wild bulls, a desperate girl, and an unpredictable kid. I thought of that old Allman Brothers song when I finally closed my eyes at night. *"It ain't over yet."*

Chapter Sixty:

Wendell

My hand was still throbbing when the fight prep guy tried to wrap some leather straps around it once we got to the arena at noon. *Handwrap.* The stuff they used before someone invented boxing gloves. I was sitting on a special bench that was wedged between two corrals. One for the stinking black bulls and the other for the white ones. Apparently the bulls got to stay in the arena and watch the fight. Too bad they didn't care. They were more interested in swishing the flies off of their butts. Across from me, the other sucker was getting his hands wrapped, too.

The arena was packed. Same as the last two days. This time we didn't have to march around waving banners. My stomach rumbled as the guy continued to wrap my hands. Once again, all I managed to choke down at breakfast was a piece of bread and some juice, even though they set out the usual platters of dried fish, dried fruit, fresh fruit, and their version of cheese.

Yidini told me that my opponent and I would be the only ones marching around the arena today. We had to walk close to the edge so that the spectators could reach out to us. I hoped that by "reaching out," he meant wishing us well and not spitting on us or doing some other bizarre thing. It didn't matter. I had worse problems. In a few minutes, I was going to get my guts ruptured by the other guy because I couldn't throw a punch with a hand that was painful to move.

I stared past the platform in the middle of the arena wondering if Aeden was at that side of the ring. Hard to tell. Next thing I knew, cymbals started clanging from all over the place and these acrobats came out of nowhere and began to tumble and somersault in front of us. Running and tumbling. Standing and tumbling. Tumbling over each other. Running and tumbling over each other until they walked to the front of the platform, bent their heads down and left.

The guy who wrapped my hands nudged me and I stood up. I looked over my shoulder and my opponent was standing, too. Yidini was right. The kid *was* tall and muscular. I turned away. No sense making myself a nervous wreck. I had plenty of time to do that once the fight got started.

The kid and I were led to the edge of the arena with me in front. Then, with one final clang of the cymbals, we began to walk the perimeter. People leaned over and touched our arms, our heads, our shoulders . . . anything that could be touched above the waist. They did this while they were screaming and yelling. *Eat your heart out Justin Bieber.*

I inched my way forward hoping that by some miracle the volcano would explode or at the very least, the bulls would get out. Neither of those things happened. Something worse did. I was halfway around the ring when I could see Aeden leaning forward and mouthing something to me. I squinted and tried to make out what she was saying. Something about *DEAD.*

Well, that helps. DEAD. Yeah, I know I'm about to be dead. Do something!

I watched and waited for her to mouth it again. Closer this time. My opponent and I were inches from her face when I saw what she was saying. Too bad she said it too late.

"SPIDER! DEADLY SPIDER! STEP BACK!"

Next thing I knew, that same unbalanced girl from yesterday leaned over, opened some sort of jar and tossed it at us. The spider bounced off my arm and then fell to the ground where it lay dead. I stepped on it just to be sure and mouthed back, "What the heck?" before moving on.

The crowd was getting louder and louder as we finished circling the arena. Within minutes

I was standing in the middle of the platform facing my opponent and wondering if I wouldn't be better off quitting and getting trampled by the bulls. As it turned out, I didn't have much time to think about it. The guy sent a quick straight punch to my shoulder and I wondered if I could deliver an uppercut to his jaw with my left hand.

No time like the present, Dell T. Do it! Just freakin' do it!

I listened to the insane voice in my head and next thing I knew I landed a straight punch to the bottom of his jaw. Best cross ever. *Hey, Junior Boxing League, how do you like that?* My opponent was unfazed and came at me with enough jabs and hooks to set a world's record. I had all I could do to slip, turn, and block. Meanwhile, the audience had gotten so loud that it all meshed into some sort of groaning roar that bombarded my senses.

Didn't matter. I had to keep punching. No one was going to blow a whistle. No one was going to do anything. *Fight to the death.* That's what Yidini said. *Got news for all of you—I don't want to kill anyone. I don't care how barbaric you guys are. Crap. You make the Romans look like a bunch of pansies.* Whoosh! I barely missed that punch.

Sweat was pouring off of me and my arms were giving out. I thought it was never, and

I mean, NEVER, going to end. If the fist throwing wasn't bad enough, an incessant buzzing began to ring in my ears. *Terrific. I wonder what kind of damage my body's taken from this beating.*

I was bracing for the next assault from the guy when all of sudden, he let out this yell and turned away from me to grab his butt! I clipped him behind his ear before I even knew it and that's when I found out why he turned around in the first place. It was a damn horsefly and it was about to land on my neck! Those stinking things carry a mean bite. The hell with Aeden's dead spider, this thing was about to do me in!

Chapter Sixty-one:

Kitane

I wanted to be stomped on the ground like that spider. It was over. I couldn't kill the contender or the *gift*. All I could do was watch the fight and wait for my father to make a betrothal announcement at the end of the Taurokathapsia.

Ariadnh, the girl and I moved away from the edge of the rink and started to walk towards the stairwell that led to our seats. We stopped for a minute to watch the fight. It made no difference to me who won. I would become someone's bride.

Both contenders were throwing punches at each other and moving around that platform so fast it was impossible to tell which one was which. I stopped looking for a second to wipe my eye and when I stared again, I couldn't believe what I saw. Their arms were waving; they were ducking their heads and throwing their fists everywhere.

A punch to the stomach, a fist to the chest, a blow to the face. They resumed the fight but something was wrong. I was about to tell Ariadnh that I thought someone might have cast a spell on them when the girl grabbed me by the arm and yanked me forward. I couldn't understand what she was saying over the noise in the arena, but she started to run into the corridor towards the section that held the bulls.

I raced behind her with Ariadnh at my heels, hoping the girl had a plan of her own to save us.

Chapter Sixty-two:

Aeden

I tried to warn Wendell not to get near that spider but it didn't matter. The thing was DOA. Probably never lived through the night. He mouthed something back to me as if this whole fiasco was my fault and the next thing I knew, Wendell was halfway around the ring and the girl with the spider was hysterical.

She was gasping, crying, and rubbing her eyes. I supposed that if I was being forced to marry Wendell, I'd be doing the same. That is . . . *if* Wendell survived. The girl and her slave started to walk back to their seats and then paused for a minute to watch the fight begin. I stood there with them, feeling absolutely useless.

Directly across from us were the corrals, packed to capacity with the bulls. At least they'd get a break today. Unlike the other days, they weren't so closely guarded. I guessed that even the centurions and the guards were too preoccupied watching the final fight to bother concerning themselves about the bulls.

It was fist after fist. Punch after punch. I winced and closed my eyes trying not to look closely at Wendell. At times, I even let my mind drift back to the images I saw on the main courtyard walls. The dolphins, the volcanoes, the bulls, even the fight and the bucolic wedding celebration. How could we possibly have landed in this bizarre civilization?

I looked up at the platform and it was as if a firecracker had gone off in my head. I remembered something from that mural that I hadn't processed before. At first glance, it appeared like a large boulder on the ground behind the man with the bloody loincloth. *No artist paints boulders like that. Use your brain Aeden.* It came to me in a flash. It wasn't a boulder. It was a man. A dead man. This was a fight to the death!

Without wasting a second, I grabbed that girl by the arm and started to yell. It didn't matter that my words made no sense. She couldn't have heard them anyway above the noise of the crowd. I ran as fast as I could out of the ring and into the corridor. The girl and her slave were right behind me. There was only one way to get Wendell out of this and I was about to do it.

Chapter Sixty-three:

Kitane

The girl was running so fast that I kept losing my breath. We were now on the other side of the arena, near the bulls. The fight was still going on in front of us and the crowd was getting louder and louder. I had no idea what that girl was about to do until I saw her make the first move. Then, Ariadnh and I did the exact same thing. Quickly. Our fingers unlatched the wooden gate and we swung it wide open. Then the next gate and the next.

The girl had already opened the wider gates where the white bulls were standing. It was just a matter of time. The bulls would rush out and fill the arena. Only they didn't. They just stood there, wiping off the flies with their tails.

Chapter Sixty-four:

Aeden

The girl and her slave were fast. In a matter of seconds we had opened all of the corrals. I had expected a furious stampede like the kind I'd seen in every Western movie since I was kid. Only it didn't happen. The bulls refused to move. I glanced around me hoping we hadn't been seen yet and I was right. Everyone was intent on the fight.

For the life of me I couldn't figure out how to get those bulls moving. I was standing in front of the largest corral, the one with the white bulls, while the girl and her slave were a few feet away with the smaller black bulls. *This never happens in rodeos. The bulls just start charging and bucking the minute the guy lets them out of the chute. Think Aeden, think! What does that guy do?*

It hit me all at once. Slap them on their rear! "WHOA!" I yelled, loud enough for the girl to hear me as I leaned over and gave one of the bulls a slap with the palm of my hand. My skin burned like it was on fire but the bull moved. It moved so fast that it butted against another bull and before I knew it, the white bulls were rushing into the arena.

The girl and her slave started to do the same thing. In a matter of seconds, the bulls were charging out like it was a scene from a John Wayne movie. Four corrals. Numerous bulls. Suddenly, the fight was no longer the focus of anyone's attention.

It was pandemonium. The yelling and cheering from the crowd turned to frantic shouts and screams. Guards, slaves and citizens-with-a-death-wish were all running into the arena to control the situation. Now was my time. There would be no other. I had to get Wendell out of there. I looked up at the platform, expecting to see him, but all I saw was an empty space. A large, square, empty space high in the middle of the arena.

Chapter Sixty-five:

Wendell

I was swatting at the stupid horsefly with one fist and trying to land a punch with the other. My opponent was no better off, except for the fact that his right hand wasn't throbbing because he probably wasn't up all night having nightmares. I swung, I ducked, I got in a few jabs and doubled over when he landed his fist in my gut more than once.

The more I sweated, the more that fly was in my face. At one point I tried to use my forearm to wipe my brow but as soon as I lifted it, my mouth could feel the leather from that guy's handwrap. It was brutal. *Junior Boxing League follows the rules, you morons!*

I just kept punching. By now, my ears were numb to the rumbling of the crowd. I heard that people who lived near subway stations never noticed the noise after a while. I could see why. The mind just has to block out some things and I guessed noise was the easiest.

The rumbling came in waves as I continued to fight. The audience was as bloodthirsty as they could get and we were giving them every reason to shout their lungs out. All at once, it changed. Not a roar anymore but a series of high pitched shrieks and screams. Then, a pounding on the ground like the earth was giving way.

Holy Crap! Did one of those damn volcanoes erupt?

My opponent felt it, too, and held off long enough for me to turn my head. It was unbelievable. Un-freaking believable! The bulls had gotten out and were charging all over the place. Without wasting another second, I spied a narrow clearing off to my right, jumped down from the platform and made a run for it. The bulls hadn't reached that part of the arena yet and neither had the guards.

I ran past the empty seats, into the corridor and out the nearest gate when it dawned on me that this was no coincidence. Someone let those bulls out and I knew who that someone was. Aeden said she'd come up with a plan all right; but I didn't think she'd base it on the Baha Men's rap, "Who Let the Dogs Out."

She had to be over by the corrals. That was only a few yards behind me and so far, no one was in the corridor. I bit the loose knot that held my handwrap together and yanked the things off of me, throwing them on the ground.

It was a thunderstorm in the arena without the lightning or the rain. I could see it as I raced through the corridor to the section that opened near the corrals. I didn't have much time. Someone was bound to recognize me and by then it would be too late.

Chapter Sixty-six:

Aeden

It was a mob scene in front of me. The girl and her slave were motioning for me to get into the corridor and away from the madness, but I couldn't leave without Wendell. If I had any chance at all of finding him, I knew I had to get to an upper story of the arena and look out.

I pointed to the stairwell behind me and took off, wondering how on earth I'd spot him in the chaos that was once the arena. Slapping my sandals onto the stone stairs, I kept climbing until I was almost at the second story. Below me, I could hear someone running. It had to be the girl and her slave. No one else was in the corridor.

Not bothering to look at first, I continued to take another step. Then, just to be sure, I looked down. Charging towards the corrals was Wendell.

"Up here! Up here!" I yelled, hearing my voice for the first time in days. I couldn't tell from the expression on his face if he was relieved or aggravated. His emotional state of mind was the last thing I was worried about. That was my mistake.

Apparently Wendell Tyler Banton was on the verge of having a major meltdown in the middle of a corridor that was about to fill up with a frenzied crowd. I spun around and practically flew down the stairs.

"Wendell, we've got to get out of here. NOW! Run for the first open archway and keep going!"

Like those idiotic bulls, he refused to move.

"Run? Run? You expect me to run? In case you haven't noticed, I'm all black and blue. For all I know, I might even have a perforated intestine!"

"You'll wish you had a perforated intestine if you don't get moving! I mean it! Look around! No, don't waste time looking around. Run! Run! Out that archway! To the harbor! Run!"

Wendell didn't have to turn around. He could see the crowd coming from all sides, including the stairwell above us. He took off and didn't look back. I was inches behind him and almost out of the archway when someone bumped into me with so much force that I stumbled forward and landed flat on the ground. The only thing I could see were dozens of sandaled feet as they ran past me.

Chapter Sixty-seven:

Wendell

I'm blaming you if my lungs explode, Aeden.
I didn't stop to catch my breath until I ran past three winding streets with those white houses. Don't let anyone tell you that running downhill is easy. They're full of it. My legs were about to collapse and everything was getting blurry. "I've got to stop and take a break," I yelled, turning back to Aeden. Only there was no Aeden.

How could someone disappear when they're right behind you? That entire arena was about to spill out on the streets any second and for all I knew, it might even include a *running of the bulls* for this whacked out place. Damn it! Where the heck was Aeden?

I knew she said something about the harbor but maybe I heard her wrong. *I hate you, Aeden. I hate you. Now I'm going to have to run back uphill to find you. Who's the responsible adult now?*

The whitewashed houses had shoulder high stone walls in front of them. I decided to make my way uphill from inside those walls so no one would see me. It wasn't as if anyone was home watching the event on TV and looking out their windows from time to time. I trudged uphill keeping my eyes fixed on the street. Either Aeden was taking her time or taking another route to the harbor.

Talk about frustration. If I kept running downhill, she'd be off her rocker that I didn't wait for her and if I waited for her and she took another street, she'd go ballistic that I didn't listen to her in the first place. I figured I was better off backtracking and for once in my life, I was right.

Aeden was practically flying down the street, that ridiculous skirt whirling around like a flamenco dancer and her hair all wild and weird. If it wasn't for the fact that there were at least five or six people on her tail, I would have been laughing my brains out.

Her voice shot out at me like a cannonball.

"WENDELL! What the heck are you waiting for? A written invitation? Run to the harbor!"

Chapter Sixty-eight:

Aeden

The harbor was our only chance and we hadn't even reached the halfway point between the arena and the docks. I just hoped we'd have enough stamina to make it. Wendell didn't stop to argue. He forged ahead, turning around once in a while. I wasn't sure if he was checking to see that I was right behind him or gauging the distance between him and the growing throng of people behind us.

I didn't think we were being chased but I wasn't about to stop and find out. I figured the crowd would dissipate once people reached their own homes. What I hadn't stopped to consider was the fact that many of them arrived by boat and they were heading to the docks as well.

My stomach was beginning to cramp from all the running and I could tell that Wendell was slowing down, too. I caught up with him as soon as we entered the marketplace.

"Listen up," I said. "There's not much time. If the angle of the sun dips down much further, we won't be able to flip back today."

"OK, do it! Do it now!"

"In case you haven't noticed, I don't have a prism or a mirror or anything reflective, we've got to keep moving till we get onto the longest dock."

"Like how's that going to help?"

"Look up! That harbor beacon is reflective and it's emitting some sort of energy. We've got to line ourselves up with the right angle of the sun and that means we've got to be at the furthest point on the longest dock. No time to waste. Move it!"

We blew through the marketplace before I knew it and raced across the dock. The angle of the sun was still holding but we didn't have much time. Oily black streaks were running down my cheeks from the hair preparation that I endured. It was the least of my problems.

Ahead of me, Wendell was at the end of the dock, staring at the beacon. Suddenly, I remembered something. *Without the vibrations we'd wind up in Santorini, not Boston.* Worse yet, we'd wind up deep underwater because the spot that we were standing on might very well have been wiped away by the island's volcanic blast a thousand or more years from now.

It didn't destroy Atlantis, Wendell, but it might destroy us.

Chapter Sixty-nine:

Wendell

Aeden had this stunned look on her face like someone who dropped their lines on opening night. I yelled at the top of my voice.

"What? What's wrong? No one's here yet. Let's do it!"

"We forgot about the vibrations. We won't be able to move horizontally in time. We'll probably drown!"

"Isn't there something we can do? Like jumping up and down on the dock?"

"The only thing that will happen is that we'll loosen the planks and fall through."

She looked down at one of the smaller fishing boats tied up next to us. I could see dead fish drying on rows of rope but the odor hadn't gotten to me yet.

"Don't tell me you want us to jump in there and start rowing, do you?"

"Well, what plan are you going to come up

with because---"

Just then, a big splash of water slapped her across the face. It was one of those large dolphins that had jumped straight out into the air and back.

"It must be after the fish," I said.

"That's it! That's it! The fish! The fish! OH MY GOD, WENDELL, DELL, whatever! This might work!"

"What? What might work?"

Aeden was more jittery and nervous than usual as she motioned for me to get closer to the boat.

"Those dolphins don't swim alone. There's got to be at least a dozen or more here. If they all start jumping at once, we'll have the vibrations we need from the water. Hurry up, lean over, grab some fish and start throwing. Don't stop!"

Aeden and I heaved those dead fish all over the place and watched as the dolphins jumped higher and higher. More fish. More dolphins. Lots of water splattering and enough vibrations in the air. We were standing in a direct beam of sunlight that passed through the beacon but had no idea if the angle was the right one.

"How many degrees between the beam and the horizon?" she screamed.

"Like I would know? Who the heck carries a protractor around with them?"

"OK, OK, move closer to me and keep your eyes on the beacon!"

We were so busy tossing fish and watching the angle of the sun that we didn't look over our shoulders to the dock behind us. Not right away, anyhow; and that was a good thing or I would have freaked out on the spot. It was the nutcase girl. The one who had the guards all in a tizzy the first day in the arena. The same girl who tried to kill me with a deadly snake and a poisonous spider. A real charmer. And now she was inches away from her next move. For the life of me, I couldn't imagine what she was going to hurl at me next.

Chapter Seventy:

Aeden

I was desperately trying to calculate distance and angles in my mind when the girl's voice came at us like a hurricane. Wendell and I were speechless. I had no idea what she wanted or why she followed us to the docks. By now my hair was dripping wet and the black goo was streaming down my neck and shoulders.

The angle of the sun wasn't going to stay in place for much longer. It was still bright enough to cast a warm beam on my face and I kept blinking as I watched the girl move closer towards us. Her slave was a few yards behind her.

"Hang on, Dell," I said. "We're about to flip back and . . ."

I never got to complete my thought because the girl jumped the dock and was inches from me. She reached out as if she was about to hug me and then, without warning, looked up at me, shrieked and shoved me back until I was teetering on the edge of the dock. What could have possibly scared her like that? A hand grabbed my shoulder and for a second I wasn't sure if it was Wendell or the girl. Then, the angle of the sun changed and the two of us were left whirling into nothingness.

Chapter Seventy-one:

Kitane

The arena was in complete chaos with bulls running everywhere and people screaming their lungs out. It was over. The Taurokathapsia was done. No winners. No victors. No suitors. The people who were seated on the top floors didn't dare move but those who were below, near the ring, raced through the corridor, out the closest gates and onto the streets.

Mother and Father remained with the royal families watching the ring explode into a mass of confusion and disorder. It would be hours before they would be able to return to the villa. That gave me the time I needed to run after the girl and thank her. She had darted ahead of us past the corridor that opened onto the streets. I yelled to Ariadnh, pointed to where the girl had gone and ran after her.

I expected the girl to go back to the villa. She had nothing to fear now. Her betrothal would be postponed as well as mine. Instead, she was headed to the center of the city and the harbor. Was she planning to escape on one of the boats? I pushed myself to move as fast as I could. Ariadnh did the same.

We weren't alone. Frenzied people who had witnessed the spectacle in the ring were also running down the streets, presumably back to their own houses or maybe the marketplace. I could hear the thud of feet pounding behind me. It was madness but I had to catch up with that girl.

Ahead of me, I could see her running, her skirt spinning wildly and her hair becoming undone. Then, from out of nowhere, I saw her joined by one of the contenders. It was hard to tell which one. Did she have a suitor all along and didn't want an arranged marriage? Was that why she helped me?

She moved through the marketplace without stopping once to catch her breath. The boy was right next to her but both of them were too far off to hear me shout. Ariadnh and I kept going.

We could see them running across one of the docks and I was certain they were going to get on a boat. A bright sunbeam narrowed in on them as I got closer. All of sudden I could see movement behind them. The dolphins! The dolphins were jumping up and down as if they had caught the energy from the arena.

I was only a few yards from where they were standing and used every bit of strength I had left from running to jump across the dock. Finally, I could thank her. I held out my arms and looked up. The image I saw frightened me to the bone. The color was draining from her hair and the sun revealed who she really was—the demon girl. That wasn't all. Next to her stood the *gift*.

Panicked, I gave her a shove and in that instant, I was swept into a dizziness that totally engulfed me.

Chapter Seventy-two

Wendell

I hope this doesn't turn out to be a thing with me, attracting nutcase girls, that is. This one was the worst. She came at us like something you'd expect to see in a horror movie. Flailing, screaming, shrieking, I tried to shove her out of the way just as she was going after Aeden but everything got screwed up.

Aeden lost her balance, I was barely keeping mine, and that girl was moving into our beam of light. The last thing I remembered was latching on to someone's shoulder but I couldn't tell who.

It felt as if my body was being stretched in a zillion directions while it was spinning through space. *Don't you dare puke on yourself Dell T. That's so uncool.*

What if it wasn't Aeden's shoulder I grabbed and I took the crazy girl into the 21st century with me? *OK, you can puke now.*

The spinning and whirling turned into a cold,

rolling sensation with so much pressure on my body that all I could do was grit my teeth and hope they didn't break off from the amount of pressure they were getting.

I braced myself for more pressure but felt the opposite. All of sudden, my body was wrapped in a cloudlike substance and for the first time, I could actually smell the air. It stunk. Like a moldy basement.

We had moved in time but I wasn't sure where, when, or with who. I was lying face down on some gushy material and probably suffering from frostbite.

Chapter Seventy-three:

Aeden

I must have jabbed my elbow into the wall as time caught up with us. The pain seared through me like a laser and then dissipated. As I stood up, I realized we were stage left near the corridor that led to the dressing rooms. Someone was giving directions out front, in the auditorium, and their voices carried backstage.

Wendell had landed face first onto a pile of billowy material that we used for the genie's dance routine. I should have been that lucky. As I rubbed my elbow, I could hear him grumbling.

"I'm freezing my tail off! Can't they afford to heat this place?"

It was hard trying not to burst out laughing, but looking at Wendell with nothing on except a loin cloth, made it difficult. Then, I realized something. What if that girl had come back with us?

"Dell, is it just us? You and me? Not the girl?"

He stood up and looked around while

I checked the immediate area, too.

"You mean the whack job who tried to kill me? No, I don't see her. What do you think happened to her?"

"Time couldn't pull her forward. We were displaced from *our* time and nature brought us back. I don't think she ever left her island. Listen," I whispered, in case someone else was near the stage, "hurry up and get into a dressing room. Look for jeans and a shirt. We've done productions of *West Side Story* and *Rent* so it shouldn't be too difficult. Same thing with sneakers. Leave your sandals and clothing in the bin marked *Laundry,* and make it quick. I can already hear voices coming from the auditorium."

"Then what?"

"Then you report for rehearsal. That's what."

"You're making me rehearse after all I've been through? I was nearly killed!"

"Yeah, well, if you want it to stay at *nearly*, you'll hurry up."

Wendell muttered something that I preferred not to repeat and did as I said.

The digital clock near the computer system behind the stage read "8:15 a.m."—less than five minutes before Ed Millington would start the rehearsal. I raced into the women's dressing room where I had stashed my street clothes and did the fastest costume change in the history of theater, even managing to tie a scarf over my head to hide my hair. I'd explain that I felt better and arrived after all to conduct the rehearsal.

I placed the skirt and bodice that I was wearing in the laundry bin and put the sandals on the shelf with the other footwear. For an instant, I wanted to touch it to remind myself where we had been but there wasn't any time.

Wendell caught up with me as I walked down the steps on stage right into the auditorium. Ed Millington was just turning on the houselights when Wendell spoke.

"This is so freakin' weird. It's like nothing happened but everything did."

"I know. Time seems to return us close to the moment when we left."

"I really wanted to see Atlantis."

"For the last time, Dell, there *is* no Atlantis. You saw the most amazing Minoan civilization. One that historians can't even fathom. Let it go at that."

"It's Dell, Dell T. And how can I let it go? I was about to be sacrificed, had to jump a bunch of bulls and then fight in the arena like it was Ancient Rome!"

I groaned as I looked at the kid.

"Fine, Dell T. You had a bad day. Drop it."

"Places! Places!" Ed Millington's voice echoed in the empty auditorium. "Oh, Aeden.

I didn't see you there. Boy, you look awful! Are you sure you should be here?"

"It's OK. I feel a bit better but you should conduct today's rehearsal. I need to go over a few things with Dell."

As Ed called the cast and crew to the front of the stage, Wendell and I stepped into the hallway. I wasted no time speaking.

"Don't you *ever,* and I do mean *ever,* do this again. I swear I'll track you down and send you straight back to that arena. And don't think I won't. Time travel is far too dangerous. Do you understand?"

"Yeah, sort of . . ."

"Look Wendell, er, Dell, I know you're smart enough to make the formulas work. It's not enough. Especially if you pull a stunt like that on your own."

"What if I'm not alone?"

"Don't tell me you're actually considering doing this again and taking some poor unsuspecting person with you?"

"No, but I was thinking that maybe you'd want to try it again."

I closed my eyes, took a deep breath, and put my hands on the kid's shoulders.

"Do not take this as a *yes.* Listen carefully. When you get older, say five or six years from now, and you are still itching to find Atlantis or whatever crazy civilization you think existed, call me, email me or send me a carrier pigeon. Until that time you've got to promise you won't use those formulas. Do I have your word?"

"Yeah, I suppose I can wait."

"Good. Then we're all set. Come on, Ed's waiting."

"Are you kidding me? I'm exhausted. Hungry. Tired . . ."

"Oh, and I'm not? Move it, Dell, I mean it."

Then, I had second thoughts. "Okay, we can make a quick stop in the lobby for all the junk food you can find in the vending machines. I always keep some spare change in my locker backstage."

"You're okay, Miss Aeden, but I want you to know it's a dorky play and you would have liked Atlantis."

"You can call me Aeden," I said as we walked to the lobby, "And yeah you're right. I would have liked Atlantis."

Epilogue:
Kitane, Akrotiri, Four Months Later

I am no longer angry at the demon girl for stealing the *gift*. I was in her clutches, too, but she let me go. I could feel the intense pull into darkness and wind before she released me. Ariadnh had to drag my body from the dock, afraid that I would be swept away again if I remained so close to the water.

"It was breathtaking and horrific all at once," Ariadnh said. "A hundred beams of light turned every color of the rainbow until the sky and the waters were one. Then, wind and darkness took the demon girl and the *gift* into the unknown."

It has been four months since the Taurokathapsia. We returned to our city a few days after the bulls were unleashed in the arena. Mother never knew that I was responsible. She told me that they waited hours in their seats while hay and grain were thrown into the ring to appease the bulls. Once sated, the beasts were easily led back to their corrals.

Father feared that the gods would punish us, for we could not provide them with their sacrifice or even a burnt offering. He was wrong. Rain has come in its season and the land is fertile. We have much to celebrate, and I, most of all. Father has agreed to wait until the next Taurokathapsia to find a suitor for me. I doubt he will.

Should the gods deliver another *gift* from its seas, I am certain the demon girl, in all her fury and determination, will return to steal that one as well.

THE END

Ann I. Goldfarb

ACKNOWLEDGEMENTS

This work would not be possible if it weren't for Two Cats Press and the incredible team of editors and proofreaders in Australia and the United States who constantly keep me on task. Thank you so much Ellen Lynes, Susan Morrow, Suzanne Scher, Susan Schwartz, Steve Somers, Lisa Tonks and Norma Weintraub. And a special thanks to my husband, James Clapp, who continues to encourage me every single day.

ENDNOTES

The Minoan Civilization thrived in the early part of the Bronze Age on the islands of Crete and Thera (now Santorini) in Ancient Greece. With coastal cities for trade and interior farming communities, the Minoan people developed a language similar to Greek, built monuments and structures, had advanced septic and water systems, worshipped their own gods and established a culture that historians are still struggling to understand.

What we do know about this compelling civilization is based on the fascinating artwork (frescos, ceramics) that archeologists have uncovered. Drawings of fish, birds, dolphins, and plants were prevalent. In addition, paintings of "bull-jumping," with complex acrobatic movements, were common. I utilized that theme in my novel with the contention that it was not merely a sport, but a ritual and rite of passage.

Since the Minoan language has yet to be deciphered (its only remnants appearing on Linear A and B tablets),[1] much of the Minoan civilization remains an enigma. That's what makes it so exciting for fiction authors like me.

---

[1] Linear A is the language found on a clay tablet discovered on the island of Crete at the turn of the 20th century.

Then, there is the "Atlantis" theory that leaves so much to speculation and imagination. Scientists do know that a volcano on the island of Thera erupted sometime between 1600-1627 B.C. contributing to the demise of that civilization and the beginnings of a notion that the "Lost City of Atlantis" had occupied the island.

The "works cited" are just a start for curious readers. I am certain that the truths yet to be discovered about the Minoans will be far more astonishing than any fiction.

WORKS CITED

- En.Wikipedia.org/wiki/Minoan_eruption
- Minoablog.blogspot.com
- www.ancientsites.com
- www.archaeology.about.com/od/mterms/qt/minoan.htm
- www.minoan.com
- www.minoanatlantis.com
- www.studymode.com/essays/Ancient-History-Minoans-Everyday-Life-367671.html (article by Emily Gold, August 2010)

Please note: The Ancient Minoan names found in this novel were cited from the Peiraeus Public Library at:www.peiraeuspubliclibrary.com

STUDY GUIDE FOR THE TIME STEALER

This young adult novel blends historical and science fiction. The study guide component provides teachers with differentiated questions and activities designed to develop thinking skills and promote a better understanding of this particular era in time. The study guide is reproducible for classroom use.

Chapters One–Five:

1. Why does Aeden feel she will have control of the situation when Wendell arrives to take part in the play she is directing? (Hint: Think about her past endeavors).
2. Describe Professor Heidecker in five words.
3. Do you consider Wendell's actions at his school to be malicious acts or juvenile pranks? Explain.
4. Why is Aeden certain of Wendell's whereabouts in time?
5. Why does Wendell blame Aeden when he goes back in time?

Chapters Six–Ten:

1. What do you think is going to happen to Wendell?
2. How is Aeden's reaction to her situation different from Wendell's?
3. What horrible discovery does Aeden make? Do you think her presumption is correct?
4. When does Wendell figure out what the people on the island have in store for him?

Chapters Eleven–Fifteen:

1. What are burnt offerings? Can you name ancient cultures that practiced human sacrifice?
2. What civilization was Wendell trying to reach and where did he wind up instead?
3. What do you suppose is Aeden's greatest challenge?
4. Find a map of Ancient Thera (Santorini Island) and locate Akrotiri and Thera.
5. Should Aeden have told Wendell to steal clothing for her? Explain your reasoning.

Chapters Sixteen–Twenty:

1. Describe what happened to Wendell in the marketplace.
2. Who are the "gift offering" and "the demon?"
3. Do you think Wendell will be able to escape

from the "victory parade?" Why or why not?

4. Have you ever been in a situation that you did not have control over? Explain.

5. Were Aeden's actions irresponsible by sending Wendell to the city alone?

6. Why does Kitane want to find the "demon girl" before her father does?

Chapters Twenty-one–Twenty-five:

1. In one word, describe Aeden's reaction when she sees Wendell in the middle of the celebratory parade.

2. Describe what you imagine will take place at the Taurokathapsia (Ceremony of the Bulls). Look for images on a computer search. What does this remind you of?

3. What are the similarities and differences between Wendell's experience preparing for the bull ceremony and his past experiences at summer camp? (You can choose to draw a Venn diagram in lieu of listing your responses).

4. Do you think someone will realize that Aeden does not belong in the villa?

5. Should Wendell be worried that his cloth indicated the *Blood Dance?*

Chapters Twenty-six–Thirty:

1. Why does Kitane steal saffron? * Find a recipe that uses this spice!
2. How does Aeden manage to fit in at the villa?
3. Why do Yidini and Sima think it is a great honor to receive the red cloth?
4. If you were in Kitane's place, would you sneak out of the villa? Explain.
5. What is the *water ride?*

Chapters Thirty-one–Thirty-five:

1. Who interrupts Wendell's activities in the arena and why?
2. What is the irony of the situation in the arena?
3. How did Aeden's acting skills help her? Describe.

Chapters Thirty-six–Forty:

1. Why did Aeden find it easy to apply make-up in such an ancient culture?
2. What minerals were used in ancient make-up? Are such minerals used today?
3. Why was it so important for the girls in the villa to be elaborately dressed?
4. How did the image of a giant bull's head appear in the harbor? What was it? Does it remind you of any other events?

Chapters Forty-one–Forty-five:

1. Create a menu for each of the three daily meals served at either Wendell or Aeden's villa.
2. Wendell compares himself to his aunt's dog when he gets prepped for the ceremony. Rewrite one of the paragraphs and compare him to something else.
3. What assumption does Kitane make about Aeden and why?
4. Why does Aeden's plan fail?
5. What do you think is going to happen to Wendell when he meets the bull?

Chapters Forty-six–Fifty:

1. How and why did Wendell manage to jump the bull with a tumblesault?
2. What is a mantra?
3. What plan does Kitane have to thwart the ceremony?
4. What plan did Aeden come up with?
5. What plan did Wendell think he'd try?
6. Whose plan do you think will work?

Chapters Fifty-one–Fifty-five:

1. What prevented Aeden from getting to the beach?
2. Why do you suppose Kitane thinks that Aeden is her ally?

3. How did the snake "save" Wendell in the ring?
4. Describe Kitane's relationship with her mother.
5. How does Aeden figure out Kitane's intentions?

Chapters Fifty-six–Sixty:

1. Yes or no: Kitane is resourceful. Explain.
2. What does Aeden realize when she looks at the frescos on the wall? How does this help her to understand Kitane's situation?
3. How does Wendell's experience with his junior boxing league in Connecticut help him?
4. In three words, describe Kitane's emotional state when she realizes the spider is dead.

Chapters Sixty-one–Sixty-five:

1. What horrific conclusion does Aeden reach and what does she do?
2. How do Aeden and Kitane work in tandem?
3. What does Wendell realize and what does he do?
4. Why do you suppose Wendell gets into a confrontation with Aeden?

Chapters Sixty-six–Seventy:

1. What initial problem do Aeden and Wendell face once they reach the docks?
2. What do you think happens to Kitane?

Chapters Seventy-one–Seventy-two, Epilogue

1. Describe what happened to Aeden, Wendell and Kitane.
2. Why do you suppose Aeden acted nonchalant about their return to the 21st century?
3. Do you think Wendell will use his knowledge of time travel to do this again? Explain.
4. If you were Aeden or Wendell, would you time travel? Why or why not?
5. What did Kitane think had happened on the dock and why?
6. Do you think Kitane will be forced into a marriage in another year?

Elements of Suspense

Can you find and identify elements of suspense in this novel? Look for the following: 1) Foreshadowing; 2) My Hands Are Tied; 3) I Know Something You Don't; 4) One Step Forward, Two Steps Back; 5) Cliffhangers; 6) Natural Fears; 7) Close Shaves.

ABOUT THE AUTHOR

New York native Ann I. Goldfarb spent most of her life in education, first as a classroom teacher and later as a middle school principal and professional staff developer. Writing has always been an integral part of her world. Her freelance non-fiction can be found in trade magazines for Madavor Media and Jones Publications, but her real passion is writing mystery-suspense for young adult audiences. Time travel is the vehicle she has chosen to embrace.

Ann resides with her family near the foothills of the White Tank Mountains in Arizona.

www.ingramcontent.com/pod-product-compliance
Lightning Source LLC
Chambersburg PA
CBHW051251210726
48287CB00002B/456